We hope you
renew it by

Return to Sundown Valley

Luke Dawson and his Navajo Indian sidekick, Honani, both Union soldiers, have ridden home from the Civil War. Each man yearns to return to a normal life but while they rode away to the War, things changed in Sundown Valley. Instead of peace in the valley, they face Dallas Zimmer who's consumed by greed and has a bunch of killers at his disposal. He's even claimed Luke's woman. Faced with murder, corruption and injustice, Luke rides through hostile Apache Country to face Zimmer and his gang in a final showdown. But are the odds too great?

Return to Sundown Valley

Cole Shelton

A Black Horse Western

ROBERT HALE

© Cole Shelton 2019
First published in Great Britain 2019

ISBN 978-0-7198-3023-5

The Crowood Press
The Stable Block
Crowood Lane
Ramsbury
Marlborough
Wiltshire SN8 2HR

www.bhwesterns.com

Robert Hale is an imprint
of The Crowood Press

Typeset by
Derek Doyle & Associates, Shaw Heath
Printed and bound in Great Britain by
4Bind Ltd, Stevenage, SG1 2XT

CHAPTER ONE

It was close to sundown when the sudden snarl of gunfire broke the silence of dusk and echoed over the canyon country.

Two riders, weary from their long, two-thousand-mile trek across rolling plains and mountain ranges, first by stagecoach and then in the saddle, reined their horses sharply as a second gunshot blasted from the far side of the next ridge.

Luke Dawson, dark-haired, lean and tall, let his right hand drop and rest on the scarred Peacemaker six-shooter nestling in its leather holster. His companion, a bronze-faced Navajo Indian, Lance Corporal Honani, took the precaution of lifting his Springfield army rifle from its saddle scabbard.

For a long moment they both simply sat saddle, listening as the whispering westerly wind carried the gunshot echoes away over the distant rims.

This sound of gunfire was far from welcome. Just over three months ago, the booming thunder of pistols, rifles and cannons had finally fallen silent when two generals, Ulysses S. Grant for the Union and Robert E. Lee for the

Confederate Army, signed the official ceasefire in the Appomattox Courthouse, ending the bitter Civil War that had divided America. Like many other battle-weary soldiers slowly making their way home from the fields of conflict, Luke and Honani didn't relish hearing gunfire. It brought back dark, haunting memories of war, like sudden death, cries of the wounded and dying, burying bullet-riddled comrades in shallow, unmarked graves.

'Could be a hunter,' Honani suggested hopefully.

They had seen wild deer in wilderness mountain country and lately in the deeper canyons of Utah, especially where the Snake River twisted and turned before spilling into Lake Sandpiper. Two weeks ago Luke had stalked and shot a mottled stag in a shadowy, log-filled clearing, providing fresh meat for them both for a whole week.

'Maybe,' Luke Dawson said, but he wasn't convinced.

Then, just as the gunfire echoes faded into silence, a frantic woman's scream pierced the twilight like a razor-sharp knife.

That decided it for the riders. First Luke, then his Navajo sidekick, prodded their horses into a quick trot, building swiftly into a fast lope as they climbed the westward trail to the sharp crest of the next ridge. Both their horses had been bought a month ago when the westbound stage left them in Denver, Colorado. Within the hour, the two Union soldiers had visited saleyards behind the town's blacksmith. Luke settled for a bay gelding the salesman said was named Buck. He'd had to tame Buck because the animal had a mind of his own. Honani chose a smaller horse, a shaggy brown pony not unlike the one he owned in Sundown Valley, where his people had lived for countless centuries.

Another high-pitched, terrified scream greeted them as they topped the golden-tipped ridge and momentarily halted their horses.

Below them, less than fifty paces away, was a motionless Wells Fargo stagecoach with four wide-eyed horses still in harness. A bloodstained man hung lifelessly over the driving seat. Two masked riders held a passenger at gun-point. This hapless man was dressed in a Confederate soldier's uniform, wooden crutches under his armpits, staring down the barrels of two Colt revolvers. Behind the stagecoach was an old tin-roofed wooden way station, its front door yawning wide open, creaking in the rising wind coming down from the distant mountains.

And it was from inside this way station that the woman's desperate screams rose again, only to be stifled.

'No! For pity's sake, no!' the soldier pleaded hoarsely with the two mounted outlaws. He moaned, 'She's my wife, we're just married—'

'Don't worry, soldier-boy,' the tallest bandit chuckled, his voice muffled under the bandana that masked the lower part of his face. 'She'll enjoy it once he gets started.'

The other outlaw sneered at the greycoat soldier, 'Look at it this way. You're just a useless cripple and you can't give a fine-looking woman like her what she needs.'

'You lousy bastards!' the soldier croaked.

'Button your lip,' the tall outlaw warned ominously.

'Yeah, shut up, Johnny Reb, or we'll plug you here and now and keep your woman for ourselves,' the other warned.

Luke and Honani exchanged swift glances. No words were needed. They'd been through Hell together for three and a half years and the last thing they wanted right now was a confrontation. However, the sight of this helpless man on crutches – albeit a Confederate soldier – weeping like a kid, and the sounds of a violent struggle punctuated by more terrified screams inside the way station gave them no choice.

They slid noiselessly from their horses.

Luke lifted his Colt from its leather and the Navajo checked his long rifle. The outlaws were so absorbed in their cruel mocking of the Confederate soldier, and making lewd remarks about what was about to happen to his wife, that they didn't even hear the soft tread of boots coming up behind them. Nor did they see the glint of hope light up the soldier's eyes as he glimpsed the two men approaching.

'Drop your guns or we'll blast you to Hell.'

Luke's command froze the bandits to their saddles.

The tallest outlaw, who'd been about to taunt the crippled soldier again, turned his head slowly and looked straight down the naked barrel of Luke's six-shooter, which had been pointing square at the centre of his back. He switched his glance to the Indian whose Springfield rifle was raised and ready, aimed straight between the other outlaw's shoulders. There was no way either of them could turn in their saddles and fire their own guns before having their spines shattered.

'Do like he says, Abe,' the tall outlaw muttered.

The tall outlaw then tossed his gun into the dust. His stumpy companion reluctantly did the same as another choking scream and the sounds of a violent scuffle came from inside the way station. There was a light-grey horse standing alongside the two mounted riders, so Luke figured there was just one outlaw inside with the woman.

'Please ... please ... help my wife,' the Confederate soldier pleaded as the sound of deep, desperate sobbing floated from the way station.

'Keep these sidewinders covered, Honani,' Luke said. He added, 'If they even look like making a move, shoot to kill.'

'This I will do with pleasure,' the Indian said resolutely.

Luke strode past the bandits and stagecoach, then barged through the door.

That's when he saw the way station owner, a balding old man with a long grey beard, sprawled motionless over his office desk, blood soaking through the dime novel he'd been reading. There was a bullet hole between his eyes.

Luke pushed through the ransacked office into a narrow passageway leading to five small rooms. It was where stagecoach passengers could sleep for the night while horses were rested. He heard a grunt, then the sounds of material being ripped and what sounded like fists pummelling flesh.

The door of the first room was ajar.

Luke pushed it open wide and saw a big, bulky man who had a struggling woman pinned to the mattress on a narrow bunk bed. Mouthing obscenities, he was ignoring her flowing tears and desperate pleas, his huge knees rammed into her belly as he shredded her dress.

'Get off her,' Luke commanded from the doorway.

With his huge knees still digging into his prey's quivering stomach, the outlaw turned sharply and saw Luke standing with his gun levelled.

'You heard me! I said get off her!' Luke repeated coldly.

'Keep your shirt on, mister,' the outlaw said softly. He

figured this stranger in the Union uniform must have been resting up in one of the rooms. There was no way he could have sneaked past his two fellow outlaws. After all, he'd just left them right outside the way station front door. He smirked, 'Look, you can have your turn, too . . . after me, of course.'

Luke pulled his trigger. Thunder rocked the way station and a bullet burned like a fiery poker into the flabby flesh of the outlaw's right buttock. Yelping in excruciating pain and hot fury, the outlaw clawed for his own holstered gun. He dragged the Colt .45 clear from its holster, but Luke's next bullet blasted him clean off the bunk. He lurched sideways into a small wooden cupboard, splintering the door from its hinges. Bleeding through his ribcage, he crashed back against the log wall. He was dead before he pitched headfirst to the floor.

The soldier's wife, who was much younger than her man, clutched the torn remains of her floral dress to her trembling body, although the shredded pieces of material barely covered her.

'Thank you! Oh, thank you! The filthy swine was about to—' Breasts heaving tumultuously, she broke into a bout of uncontrolled sobbing. She was still weeping as she blurted out, 'My husband . . . Is he—?'

'He's alive and well, ma'am,' Luke put her mind at rest as he sheathed his gun. 'My saddle pard has the two other hold-up men at gunpoint.'

'Praise God,' she said fervently.

'I'm needed outside, ma'am,' Luke said. 'I suggest you hunt around and see if the way station owner has spare clothes stashed away here. Mightn't exactly fit you but they'll be better than nothing.'

10

'Mister, I have clothes,' the woman told him quickly. 'They're in my luggage, the brown case strapped to the stagecoach roof. My husband and I were on the way home from our honeymoon when the stagecoach was held up, you see. The bandits were staked out here in the way station waiting for us.'

'There's a bed blanket in there,' Luke Dawson said, indicating the smashed cupboard. 'Wrap it around yourself so you're decent.'

'Yes, of course,' she said gratefully.

'Meanwhile, I'll fetch your case.'

As Luke turned to leave, she said fervently, 'My man fought for the Confederacy, and by the uniform you're wearing you're a Union soldier, but I'm sure beholden to you, mister.'

'War's over, ma'am,' he reminded her.

'Yes, thank God,' she agreed.

Luke headed back through the way station office to the open door.

While Luke was inside, Honani had ordered the outlaws to dismount and now they stood unmasked, hands in the air, with their backs flat against the way station wall. The Confederate soldier had reached up and grabbed the dead stage driver's gun and now he leaned on his crutches right next to the Union lance corporal, blue and grey uniforms side by side together.

Luke gave the bandits a cursory glance as he reached up to unstrap the woman's travelling case from the stagecoach roof. The taller outlaw had a lean, wolfish face with long teeth like rotting fangs and a deep crimson scar running down his right cheek. He was muttering profanities under his breath. His younger companion, stout and shifty-eyed,

11

had a prominent nose, thick lips and a jutting jaw. Both their faces sprouted dark stubble.

Luke unstrapped the case. After a brief word with Honani, he carried the case inside where he found the woman waiting, now wrapped in a thick but moth-eaten woollen blanket.

'Thank you,' she said again, opening her case.

Leaving her to get dressed, Luke returned outside.

There he joined Honani and the Confederate soldier, three guns together, all ready to shoot if necessary.

'I'm Major Timothy Wallace,' the grey-coated soldier said, introducing himself to Luke and Honani. The Navajo lance corporal raised his thin black eyebrows at hearing the crippled man's rank. Wallace added, 'Just call me Tim. Thanks for horning in, gentlemen. I certainly owe you.'

'So what do we do with these murdering skunks?' Honani asked.

'I suggest we hang them from that tree,' Wallace drawled, nodding to the tall Bristlecone pine that overshadowed the way station.

The tall outlaw's face turned ashen suddenly, while his companion trembled like a leaf in a storm.

Luke let them sweat for a moment before declaring, 'A necktie party's what they deserve, but we'll take them to the sheriff of Spanish Wells and let the town hangman do the chore.'

Clouds edged slowly across the face of the full moon, and a chill wind whistling down from the canyons stirred the sagebrush outside the way station. The major's wife, introduced by him as Mrs Elizabeth Wallace, sat inside beside the wood stove, watching the deer steak sizzle in the black frypan on the single hot plate. On the table stood the coffee pot that had just been warmed. Elizabeth was a fine-looking woman, Luke observed. Curly honey-blonde hair, tall and shapely, she was obviously very much in love with her Confederate husband. Wallace was indeed a lucky man, Luke decided, especially when the major, sharing cigars with the soldiers, proudly said this young and beautiful woman had loyally waited all of four long years for him to return from the war.

Right then, Luke thought about Sierra Cooper, the girl he'd left behind in Spanish Wells. It had been two long and lonely years since her last letter. She was the town's school-ma'am, with long raven-coloured hair, tall and willowy, pretty as a picture. Luke used to come calling when he'd been in town, but the war had interrupted their courtship.

Her whispered promise, 'I'll wait for you', had kept him going during the darkest hours of the bloody conflict.

As they waited for supper, Wallace lamented, 'A blue-coat soldier, just a kid, probably sixteen years of age, maybe even younger, put a bullet in each knee instead of killing me. Reckon I'll be on these damn crutches for a helluva long time. Hopefully not for the rest of my life.'

'At least you survived the war, unlike many,' the Navajo said.

The three former soldiers drank their coffee. The bodies had been wrapped in blankets and stacked inside the Wells Fargo stagecoach, while the captured outlaws, who finally and grudgingly admitted to the names Sam West and Abe Thompson, sat on the floor with their hands roped behind their backs. Wallace produced some tobacco, which he shared with Luke and the Navajo. Luke felt no animosity towards the major, despite the colour of his uniform. In fact, he liked the man.

'So why did you sign up?' Major Wallace asked tentatively.

'My youngest brother Wesley hooked up with a runaway slave,' Luke said as Elizabeth handed him his supper. 'Fine woman, Marigold, black as the ace of spades with a heart of gold. They planned to make a life together, but a bunch of riders hired by plantation owners to hunt down escaped slaves murdered my brother and dragged her back in chains. Spent a long time trying to track down his killers but their trail was cold. I never found them. Then when I was told the north wanted to free the slaves and the seven southern states were going to fight to keep them, that decided me. I enlisted the first month.'

There was silence between them as Luke Dawson remembered that day. He'd left his Bar LD spread in the capable hands of his older brother Caleb and wife Susan, exchanging the life of rounding up and taming wild horses for a blue uniform and the muddy fields of sudden death.

Now, like Navajo Honani, his lifelong friend, he was riding home.

They would be in Spanish Wells tomorrow. After visiting the undertaker and the sheriff, they'd ride together across Sundown Valley where Honani would be united with his Navajo people and he would ride his bay gelding up the steep mountain trail to Old Wolf Ridge.

'Well, I joined the army when I was seventeen,' Wallace told them as they all ate their steaks. 'Served at Fort Worth, then a spell with Custer. Came back to Utah where I became a major. As you know, when the Civil War broke out, some Utah soldiers joined the Union and some backed the Confederacy. We were a divided state. I fought with General Robert E. Lee until that bluecoat kid blasted holes in my knees.' He took a swig of his coffee as Elizabeth came and placed an arm around her man. He added sincerely, 'But the war's over now. I hold no grudges.'

'Neither do I,' Elizabeth reaffirmed.

'Mind you, I'll still be flying the Confederate flag outside our home when we get back,' Wallace asserted defiantly.

'Timothy!' she chided him gently.

Deciding he'd best change the subject, Major Wallace observed, 'Your Indian friend doesn't say much.'

Honani cracked a rare smile. 'Not much to say. My friend Luke Dawson went to war. I rode with him and they gave me a blue shirt.'

'He's not a man to boast,' Luke explained, 'but he was one of the few Indians to become a lance corporal. And he earned the promotion. He was braver than most. In fact, he has a medal to prove it. Show them, Honani.'

The Navajo hesitated but finally he relented and opened the top two buttons of his Union uniform. Hanging from the rawhide looped around his neck was a shiny gold star framed in a circle.

'Holy Moses,' Major Wallace exclaimed in awe.

Even his wife Elizabeth knew what it was. 'Praise be! The United States Medal of Honour!'

'We were under siege,' Luke recalled as they both stared at the Navajo's medal resting proudly against his bronze skin. 'Your Confederate soldiers had us trapped at the mouth of Grey Coyote Pass. Remember that battle? You had two Gatling guns pumping lead at us. We had twenty, maybe thirty wounded men to carry through that narrow pass to safety. Corporal Honani volunteered to stake out

15

behind a clump of rocks with half a dozen loaded rifles beside him to hold off the Johnny Rebs. We all thought he was crazy, but he was the officer in charge so we let him do it. He held his post for a full hour, allowing us to get our wounded through the pass. He received the Medal of Honour for his bravery.'

'You did not mention that once the wounded were safe, you came back to help me,' the Indian said. He added, 'However, they gave you no medal.'

'You were the one who deserved it,' Luke stated.

'We are now blood brothers,' Honani said proudly.

They had in fact been friends for many years.

When Luke and his older brother Caleb had first arrived in Spanish Wells with their wagon, they'd made their way across Sundown Valley. It was open range and the Navajos lived in their village on the bank of a swiftly flowing creek. Caleb's wife wanted to buy a Navajo shawl and they were made welcome in the village, staying the night in one of the lodges. It was there Luke met Honani, the chief's eldest son who told him about the best places to hunt in the mountains that overlooked the Indian village. Thus a friendship began. Honani was a welcome guest in the cabin Luke built and in turn the white man was treated as a brother in the village. Luke went on to build a horse wrangling spread high on Old Wolf Ridge that overlooked the valley, and more than once Honani had helped him rope and break in some mustangs. Then they went to war together, and now they were riding home.

They finished the meal Elizabeth Wallace had cooked.

'You can all get some shuteye,' Luke told them. He returned the coffee pot to the potbelly stove, looked at the outlaws and patted his holstered gun. 'I'll keep watch over these buzzards.'

It was later, when they were all asleep, that Luke Dawson made another mug of coffee. He was still thinking of the beautiful Sierra and ultimately her being with him in his home on the edge of the mountains.

They left the way station as the new sun painted the far eastern rims in dazzling golden light.

Luke rode ahead of the Wells Fargo stagecoach, with Wallace and his wife seated together on the driving seat. It had taken the major all of five minutes to painstakingly climb up there, but he was a proud man and insisted on doing it without any assistance. Wallace had the reins while Elizabeth, wedged close to her husband, had a rifle resting over her lap. The major assured Luke that Elizabeth knew how to use it and she'd relish doing so if Thompson and West tried to escape. The Navajo brought up the rear, with the horses ridden by the two outlaw prisoners roped behind the stagecoach. The bandits, Thompson and West, cussing, grumbling and eating dust, had their wrists tied to their saddle horns.

The trail snaked west, deeper into Utah. Luke knew the trail well. It was one he'd ridden many times before going to war, and had even driven horses along its dusty length. Today it was still a ribbon of deep dust, used by stage-coaches, pony express riders and pioneer wagon trains alike. Ultimately it would reach Spanish Wells, curl around Sundown Valley and probe even further west into canyon country.

Right now as they followed this winding trail, they entered a lonely pass where vultures circled high in the morning sun. Emerging from the pass, they squeezed

17

between two red buttes, then swung southwest past an old mine shaft that was no longer in use.

By late morning they reached a shallow valley. It was then that Honani left the prisoners and joined Luke ahead of the swaying stagecoach.

'We have company,' the Navajo said as they rode side by side. 'By those cottonwoods on that ridge.'

Luke's eyes narrowed as he slowed his horse. 'I see them.'

Half a dozen riders were making a motionless line on the crest of a wooded ridge that protruded like an ancient balcony just ahead over the valley trail. They were close enough for Luke to see that most of the silent riders wore leather shirts and breechcloths with high moccasin boots and headbands. One of them, the oldest, was clothed in a white Mexican tunic and cavalry pants.

'Apaches,' Honani said, confirming what he thought.

'All with rifles,' Luke observed.

'Supplied by gunrunners, that's for sure,' the Navajo said.

'Nothing has changed then,' Luke remarked.

This wasn't Apache territory. Before white settlement this had all been Navajo country, but even then Apache renegades had ridden down from their mountain strong-holds – rarely to hunt, usually to raid and kill. Many a young Navajo maiden had been snatched from her village by warlike Apache bucks, and Honani's youngest brother, Moki, out hunting alone a few years ago, had been butchered on the bank of a river by the raiders. There was no love lost between the Navajos and the Apaches.

'Reckon they'll attack us?' Luke asked.

The Navajo switched his eyes from the ridge top to a

wisp of dust arising from an arroyo that crossed the valley like a vein. 'They've set an ambush,' Honani said. As he lifted his Springfield rifle, he uttered a warning. 'Dust, just ahead past that sagebrush.'

'So they're on both sides,' Luke said.

By now Wallace had seen the Apaches on the ridge. Seated behind the reins on the driver's seat, he grabbed the rifle his wife had been holding. Elizabeth stifled a gasp of fear. She'd survived a terrifying ordeal at the hands of those outlaws but she felt even more fearful when she saw that line of Apache warriors too. The six-shooters surrendered by Thompson and West lay at her feet so she scooped them up, ready if need be to fight alongside her husband.

Luke and Honani kept riding together in front of the slowing stagecoach. They were in open country, soon to pass a looming clump of sandstone rocks. In less than a minute they would be between the wooded ridge and an unknown number of Apaches that Honani knew were staked out in the arroyo.

'We're sitting ducks here,' Luke said. 'We'll run the gauntlet.'

'Dawson!' Sam West yelled from behind the stagecoach. Both the captured outlaws were now aware of the Apaches on the ridge. He demanded frantically, 'Cut our ropes! Give us our guns back!'

'We're white men!' Abe Thompson hollered desperately. 'We have the right to defend ourselves!'

Luke ignored their squealing protests. He was more interested in getting Wallace and his wife to safety. Turning in the saddle, he motioned to the major and the terrified Elizabeth.

He told them, 'Keep your heads low, and when I give the signal get those horses moving as fast as they'll go. I want dust raised, a helluva lot of dust, then some more.'

'Good strategy, Bluecoat,' the Confederate officer complimented him, declaring loudly, 'We're ready.'

'Now!' Luke ordered.

One wiry Apache, impatient for a kill, fired his rifle from the ridge top.

The bullet thudded into the side door of the Wells Fargo stagecoach as Major Timothy Wallace flicked his whip, prodding the four wide-eyed horses into a frenzied lope that threw yellow dust into the rising sun. Apache slugs sprayed from the ridge as Luke, Honani, the Wells Fargo stage and two outlaw prisoners gathered speed and thundered down the trail. Three hostile bullets burned past Honani, two smacked into the swaying stagecoach and one splintered into the driver's seat, less than an inch from Elizabeth's hip.

The stagecoach horses gathered more speed, making thick dust billow into a swirling cloud. Eating dust at the rear, Thompson and West clung to their saddle horns as their horses were forced to gallop harder to keep up with the stage. A stray Apache bullet ripped flesh from Thompson's left arm, making him yelp like a whipped dog as flecks of blood flew from his torn shirt.

Riding just ahead of the Navajo, whose Springfield rifle had already downed one ridge ambusher, Luke glimpsed two mounted Apaches emerging from the arroyo. Both had rifles levelled. Luke shot one out of his cloth saddle and he tumbled to the ground, dead as he crashed into the dust.

The other, naked except for his breechcloth, managed

to fire a single bullet that whined harmlessly between Luke and Honani and ricocheted off a bald boulder. He levelled his rifle again as he was joined by another brave who had remained staked out in the arroyo until now. This Indian, plump and scarred from many battles, urged his pony on to the trail. The two of them began pumping lead.

With his bay horse surging forward, Luke fired twice, winging the scar-faced Apache who turned his pony and fled. Wallace took care of the other one with a single shot from the stage driver's rifle.

By now the swaying stagecoach was directly under the ridge. Riding hard alongside Luke, Honani used his Springfield to shoot a bold Apache urging his pinto pony down the ridge slope, leaving four others half-hidden by the cottonwoods on the crest. Their leader, the one dressed in the Mexican tunic, took a long, hard look at the Navajo before pumping lead. Two bullets whistled past Honani, then kicked dust on the far side of the trail. Glancing up, Honani caught a fleeting glimpse of the Apache leader's dark, angry face, a mask of bitter hatred. Firing swiftly, the Navajo soldier's bullet smacked into a cottonwood trunk inches from the Apache's skittish pony that began plunging in terror.

Then booming dust came between them. The gunfire died as Luke led the bouncing stagecoach further down the trail, out of rifle range. Reaching the mouth of Sidewinder Pass, Luke reined his horse, turned in the saddle and looked back at the ridge.

They had indeed run the gauntlet: the Apaches had gone. Accordingly, Luke gave the signal to slow down, waiting as Honani joined him. The Wells Fargo stage rolled alongside next, closely followed by the prisoners who were roped behind them. Thompson was bellowing his fury and West choking on dust that he'd swallowed. They were all coated with thick red dust that clung to their skins and clothes.

Luke knew they were now less than two hours away from Spanish Wells. All they had to do was ride through the pass, cross a bare mesa and then head down a steep slope to town.

Luke thought wryly that he and Honani had travelled around two thousand miles without hearing a shot fired in anger, yet now, almost home, they'd tangled with outlaws and had a running gunfight with hostile Apaches.

It wasn't the kind of homecoming he'd looked forward to. He hoped it wasn't an omen.

They headed into Sidewinder Pass.

CHAPTER TWO

The town of Spanish Wells sprawled below them as they rode out of the grey shadows of Sidewinder Pass. The settlement had been given its name by half a dozen Spanish Franciscan missionaries who'd travelled east from California several generations ago, trekked through canyon country, dug two wells and built a mission. They'd come to convert the Navajos and the Apaches but with limited success. Now the Spaniards had long gone, the adobe mission had become a Mormon tabernacle but their two deep, stonewalled wells still provided enough water for Main Street's horse troughs. Mostly, though, the town's water was now carted from the shallow river that spilled out of the mountains, flowed through Sundown Valley and twisted south into the canyon country.

Having emerged from the pass, Luke and Honani still rode ahead of the dust-caked Wells Fargo stagecoach as the trail crossed a crumbling mesa and began its slow decent. They headed past Pa Whittaker's trading post, noting the whiskery old timer was still sitting out front smoking a pipe, just as he had been the day they headed east to join the Union army. Old Mr Whittaker raised the same thin arm he'd farewelled them with, greeting them with a casual wave as if they'd only been away for a day.

Leaving the trading post, the riders reached the stock-yards, six of them stacked with prime beef cattle. A glance at the branded hides told him most if not all these fat beeves had come from Dallas Zimmer's Triple Z ranch, the big spread that bordered on Sundown Valley. Luke had never taken to the Zimmer crew. He'd heard that Dallas Zimmer, who'd come from Tombstone City where he'd owned a gambling den in partnership with his brother Cain, had bullied the O'Meara family into selling their land to him well below the market value. As for Zimmer's lazy, obese son, George, Luke had little regard for him either. From what he recalled, George Zimmer almost lived in the Lucky Deuce saloon and wasted most of his time there playing poker with tinhorn gamblers. His father might be a rancher, but folks used to remark that George had never punched a steer in all his twenty-nine years of life.

The dust-caked cavalcade reached town limits and started down Main Street. It was a quiet Friday afternoon. It must be music lesson time because Luke heard singing from the school and he imagined Sierra Cooper standing out the front of her class. She was an accomplished musician, playing the pedal organ for hymns every Sunday afternoon in the Spanish Wells Gospel Chapel. Luke could hardly wait to see her but he knew she'd be busy at school teaching, then tidying up after the children had left for home. He needed to give her almost an hour at least. He could wait a few extra minutes after four long, lonely years.

With the Navajo riding alongside him, Luke headed further down Main Street. They passed the town's general

24

store. According to the faded sign over his open doorway, Quaker Dale Fenwick still owned the business. Scrupulously honest, dour Fenwick and his dainty wife, who always wore a grey bonnet, were both well respected. Fenwick would probably be elected mayor one day. Next door to the general store was a clapboard building. Black curtains hung in the front window, the door was shut and a sign told all and sundry that Mister Uriah Kemp, the town undertaker, was open for business. After securing his horse to a hitching rail, Luke knocked on his door.

Kemp opened the door wide, recognizing Luke immediately. Hefty and built like a buffalo, Uriah Kemp was a former lumberman from the northern mountains who'd been enticed to become a mortician when the town undertaker, Clement D. McPherson, offered him a deal he couldn't resist. 'Go fetch some logs, build me a cabin and my undertaking business is yours.' The result was that McPherson had retired out of town, taking with him a sprightly but elderly widow whose husband he'd recently buried. Their brand new log cabin was on Wild Wolf Ridge, an hour's ride from Luke's horse wrangling spread. Now Kemp was growing a healthy bank balance as the town's sole undertaker.

'If it ain't Luke Dawson!' Kemp bellowed his welcome. 'Back from that dang crazy war!'

A lot of folks thought the Civil War had been futile and crazy: Americans killing their fellow Americans. Some men joined the Quakers in refusing to enlist. There were times when Luke had to admit they had a point.

'Howdy, Uriah,' Luke returned his greeting. 'It's good to be home.'

The mortician glanced up at Major Wallace and his wife

huddled together on the driving seat of the stagecoach. He frowned. 'Where's Jones? He's been driving this stage for ten years.'

'Jones is inside the stagecoach, Uriah,' Luke informed him. 'There are others in there too. There's the way station owner. According to his books, his name is Brett Behan. Then we've brought in an ornery outlaw skunk who, we believe, used to answer to the name of Clanton.'

'Three cadavers for you to take care of, Mr Kemp,' the major said soberly.

Uriah Kemp stomped to the stagecoach, wrenched open its right-side door and saw three blanket-clad bodies stacked between the seats. Their stench would make most folks recoil but Kemp was used to it.

'We'll help you carry them inside,' Luke offered.

'No, it's my job to look after the deceased until earth covers their pine boxes and headstones are carved and planted,' Uriah Kemp recited what he'd told countless folk who'd sought his professional services. He bent over and lifted the first body out. It was Jones, the usual stage driver. Shouldering the body, Kemp informed Luke, 'I know Nat Jones has family. Two brothers, three sisters, and a father who's still breathing. Live just south of town.' He announced confidently, 'They'll pay me my usual fee.' He carried the driver inside and returned for the other two. He paused by the parlour's open door and scrutinised them. 'As for Behan and Clanton, well, reckon the town committee will fix me up.'

When Undertaker Kemp had finished carrying the corpses into his funeral parlour, Luke remounted his bay horse.

'I'll start measuring them for coffins,' the grim-faced

26

mortician said, rubbing his long hands together.

'We'll be riding on now,' Luke told him.

Uriah Kemp had his front door partly closed as he said, 'Thanks for bringing them in.' He added warmly, 'And like I said, good to see you home.'

'I'll be really home later in the day,' Luke said. He added, 'Probably catch up with our mutual friend, Old Clem McPherson, tomorrow.'

'I don't think so, Luke,' Kemp said quietly.

'What do you mean?'

'You've been away at the war, so you wouldn't have heard about Mr McPherson. Fact is he's residing in the Spanish Wells cemetery. Third row back from the big pine. Been resting there next to his woman, Mrs Constance McPherson, for two and a half years. Helluva sad day when I buried them both the same hour, side by side. Constance first, then him, both in the best pine boxes I had. It was the least I could do.' He recalled mournfully, 'I remember it was teeming with rain too. Everyone got drenched, preacher included.'

'What happened, Uriah?' Luke asked tonelessly.

Kemp said nothing for a moment. Finally, he responded, 'You might as well hear it from me. Mr McPherson and his dear wife Constance were murdered. Both found dead in their bed with bullet holes in their heads. The holes were plumb between their eyes.'

Luke felt a coldness grip him. Clem and Constance McPherson were both his neighbours on Wild Wolf Ridge. They were good, peaceable folks, the salt of the earth, whose triple-roomed cabin had been raised ten minutes ride from his. He remembered them as likeable folks who never caused any trouble, always willing to help out if needed.

27

'Who killed them?' Luke demanded.

Uriah Kemp shrugged his broad shoulders. 'No one knows. Old Wishbone Clarkson came calling because he hadn't seen or heard of them for a fortnight, and found them dead. Not a pretty sight, he told me. The sheriff and a couple of men from town rode out and poked around but the killer had left no clues. It was cold-blooded murder, sure enough.' The undertaker muttered, 'Some mean, ugly bastard's got away with it.'

Brimming with anger but also feeling helpless to do anything after all this time, Luke asked, 'Why would anyone want to kill Old Clem and his woman?'

The undertaker shrugged his broad shoulders. 'The sheriff found no money in the cabin, Clem's gold watch was missing and so was Mrs McPherson's jewellery box, so he reckoned the motive must have been robbery. Everyone agreed with him at the time.'

'Thanks for letting me know,' Luke Dawson said. He picked up his reins. 'So long, Uriah.'

'Yes, so long,' Kemp said, still lingering in the doorway.

The town undertaker could have told him more – lots more, in fact – but maybe it was best that Luke Dawson found out for himself. And that would surely happen soon enough, Uriah Kemp told himself. He closed the door now, then reached for his measuring tape and approached his corpses. There was work to be done.

Luke and Honani prodded their mounts into a steady walk as they rode ahead of the stagecoach and their two outlaw prisoners on their way further down Main Street. Half a dozen men lounging on a wooden bench by the town's two wells and a couple of women leaving the Women's Sewing and Quilting Circle meeting in the

Mormon tabernacle stopped to watch as Luke Dawson drew level with them. The soldier had been away a long time. Onlookers noticed his face looked gaunt, there was a scar running across the top of his left cheek where a Rebel bullet had grazed him, and his hair needed a visit to the barber's shop, but several men actually recognized him, and one of the women, who used to work in Fenwick's general store, raised her arm to greet him. He was leaner, his face hardened by war, but he was Luke Dawson sure enough, the man they'd once hoped would wear the town's badge. Luke had declined the Town Committee's offer, however, and after he'd left for the war, they'd finally pinned their badge on someone else. One of the board-walk loungers recalled Navajo Honani. The old timer's pipe stuffed with tobacco fell from his cracked lips as he blinked at the lance corporal's stripes clearly visible on his dust-smeared blue tunic.

'Well, I'll be damned! The Injun's come up in the world. He's a flamin' officer!'

The two riders headed by the wells, passed the black-smith's forge and slowed their mounts by the long garish front of the Lucky Deuce saloon. The enticing smell of redeye whiskey came to them and they heard the tinkle of piano keys.

Luke was reminded it'd been a long time since he'd had a drink.

He rode by the Gospel Chapel where he'd imagined his wedding to Sierra would take place. The church was made of adobe brick, and it boasted a high belfry where a big brass bell pealed on Sundays to summon the faithful to evangelical worship, led by the Reverend Dane Tregonning.

They reached the sheriff's office, built of red canyon stone and shaded by two ancient pinions. The law office had a single barred window and Luke saw black lace curtains edge slightly apart. Someone inside was watching. Luke dismounted by the notice board, which displayed half a dozen reward dodgers. He noticed that Bill Scurlock, who'd been robbing and killing before he'd left for the war, was still on the run from the law. The reward of five hundred dollars was double what it used to be. Waiting for the Navajo to join him, Luke knocked on the door. They were greeted by a long silence before hearing the thud of heavy boots on the floor followed by the sharp grate of an iron bolt.

The door whined open and the Spanish Wells lawman stood there, his brows knitted into a frown, blinking in disbelief.

Luke had expected to see slightly built Sheriff Seth Pringle peering at them over his black-rimmed spectacles, but instead this man wearing the tin star was big, bulky and much younger. Even though the sheriff was bearded, both Luke and Honani recognized him straight away as George Zimmer, the rancher's son. Four years ago, George had boasted a young, freckled face and curly red hair. Now, however, his face was marred by two knife slashes, his nose was squashed and his hair hung like rat's tails. He looked like he'd been in a fight.

'Howdy, Dawson, so you survived the war,' Sheriff Zimmer said, without an ounce of enthusiasm in his voice. He flicked ash from his fat cigar before finally adding, 'Good to see you alive and well.'

'We both survived, same as many others did,' Luke said.

George Zimmer offered no greeting to Honani. Instead,

he looked past the Indian to the battered stagecoach, his eyes narrowing as he saw the two prisoners. 'Well, well! What have we here?'

'They gave their names as West and Thompson,' Luke said.

'We were on our way here when we came upon them holding up the stagecoach,' the Navajo explained. 'They'd killed the stage driver and way station man and terrorised passengers. So we brought them in.'

Lawman Zimmer looked at the stripes on the Indian's faded Union army uniform. 'Hmmm! Lance Corporal, huh?'

'He earned those stripes,' Luke affirmed.

Ignoring Luke's remark, Zimmer said, 'Reckon I know you, Indian.'

'We have met,' Honani said tersely. 'It was where my people live, the place white men call Sundown Valley.'

'Yeah, that's right,' Sheriff George Zimmer said with a shrug of his heavy shoulders. He folded his arms over his massive chest as his fat lips cracked a grin. 'If I remember, we had a slight disagreement at the time. It was . . . uh . . . over a woman.'

'White Lily was already promised to a Navajo buck,' Honani reminded him. 'It was not possible for you to have her.'

'I didn't plan to marry her,' the new lawman sneered derisively. 'I just wanted some fun.'

'And at the time my father sent me to say no,' Honani recalled the subsequent confrontation. 'You were not pleased but we didn't fight. You just rode away.'

'Didn't figure a bloody squaw was worth fighting over,' Zimmer dismissed the subject. He lumbered past Luke and

31

Honani, then planted his big boots beside the front of the Wells Fargo stagecoach. Puffing on his cigar, he looked up at Major Wallace and his wife. 'So, folks, what's your part in this?'

It was Elizabeth who began telling the story, her voice choking and eyes brimming with tears when she came to the part where Clanton had tried to rape her.

Mercifully, Luke interrupted her account, telling the lawman, 'Mrs Wallace shouldn't have to tell her story right here on Main Street.'

'Maybe you're right,' the lawman conceded. He ambled past the stage and appraised the two prisoners. 'I'll lock these turkeys up and you can all sign statements in the office.'

Ten minutes later West and Thompson were prodded into cells two and three that lined the western wall of the office. Cell one, in the corner behind the desk, was occupied by a white-haired oldster who was fast asleep and snoring like a pig, even at this late hour. 'Drunk and disorderly,' the sheriff explained. The lawman slumped into the chair behind his desk, shuffled through his top drawer and produced sheets of white paper.

'I want a signed statement from all of you,' Sheriff Zimmer told them. 'Neat, truthful and accurate: that's what Judge Grant Hammond will require. Then I'll charge West and Thompson with robbery and murder and whatever else I can think of.' He consulted his daybook. 'The judge arrives this Friday, so I'm expecting a double hanging following the Sabbath.'

George Zimmer walked to the open fireplace as the four witnesses used the pens and inkwells he provided to each write an account of the murders of the stage driver and way station owner. Meanwhile, the sheriff lit a new cigar in the fireplace's glowing coals and strutted over to cell one, which he unlocked.

Prodding the old timer with his boot, the lawman said, 'I'll let you off without charge this once, Monty, but next time you'll get such a helluva big fine that you won't be able to afford any more redeye for a month, which'd just about kill you. Savvy, Monty? Now git the hell out of here.'

Mumbling, old Monty stumbled past the four witnesses, wrenched open the door and staggered to a boardwalk bench.

The Navajo finished his statement first. He'd had two years of mission education but he wasn't a man of letters. Zimmer, however, read what he'd written and nodded his approval. Elizabeth Wallace completed her statement next, followed by her husband and finally Luke. Zimmer accepted them all with a grave nod, puffed on his cigar and escorted the witnesses to the front door.

'Some, maybe all of you, could be called as witnesses,' Sheriff George Zimmer declared as they walked out on to the street.

The law office door closed behind them.

'We'll be headed for home now,' Major Wallace said with his wife clinging to his right arm. He added sincerely, 'Once again, we're beholden to you both.'

'Yes, we certainly are,' Elizabeth agreed.

'Probably see you in court,' Luke said.

The two Union soldiers watched Wallace and Elizabeth walk towards their home in the narrow street across from Elva's coffee house. It was the same street where Sierra lived. By now school should be over.

'Just need to pay a visit before we ride to Sundown

Valley,' Luke said.

'No need to explain, Private Dawson,' Honani responded with a grin. 'In the meantime, I'll call into Quaker Fenwick's general store. My supplies are mighty low, and besides, I want to take some food to my people. Sort of a homecoming present,' he explained.

Five minutes later, Sheriff George Zimmer rose from his desk chair, parted the curtains and let his cold brown eyes rove Main Street. His visitors had all gone their several ways. Only the dusty stagecoach and its horses stood alone and unattended, waiting for the local Wells Fargo manager to come and collect. This could take another hour, as Zimmer knew the bald manager would right now be enjoying the ministrations of his favourite saloon girl, Avis, in her notorious 'Blue Room' in the Lucky Deuce saloon. Come to think of it, he could do with a visit there himself. It had been a whole week since he'd indulged himself.

Maybe later this evening, he decided.

'Sheriff!' Thompson summoned him.

West rattled the bars of cell two and bawled impatiently, 'Yeah, don't just stand there, George.'

Sheriff Zimmer gave them a cursory glance, pulled the curtains back and strolled to his desk, where he re-read the witnesses' statements one by one. When he'd finished, he shrugged and screwed all the statements up into a single papery ball. Humming to himself, he walked across his office. Watched by West and Thompson, he tossed the ball into the hungry flames that were licking two glowing logs. Arms folded, the lawman of Spanish Wells stood waiting as the paper caught alight, flared and was consumed until all that was left of the written statements were black fragments amidst grey smoke.

He bent over and picked up a battered coffee pot being warmed in the coals. Humming, he poured coffee into three stained mugs. After gulping down a single mouthful of his coffee, Zimmer carried two steaming mugs to his prisoners. Hands wormed through the bars to grab their drinks.

'You'll soon be out of here,' George Zimmer told them, using his shirtsleeve to polish his shiny silver badge. He appraised his two prisoners. 'I'll come back at midnight, unlock your cells and set you free.'

'Hell! Do we have to wait that long?' West snapped.

'Yeah, can't you do better than that, George?' Thompson moaned.

Sheriff George Zimmer ignored their complaining. 'I'll have two hosses saddled and ready in the law office stable out back.' He advised, 'Ride slow and quiet and straight out of town.'

'You don't need to tell us that,' Thompson said testily.

'We're not stupid,' West agreed with his fellow outlaw.

'One more thing,' the sheriff said, ignoring their mutterings, 'I'm taking a ride. Soon Deputy Drake's due back from the barber's shop and he'll be in charge while I'm gone.' He warned, 'Don't say a word out of place. Drake knows nothing – I repeat, nothing – and it needs to stay that way.'

'Sure, George, we'll keep our traps shut,' West said.

'Don't worry! We'll just sit nice and quiet, finish our coffee and have a nap,' Thompson said, yawning.

'See that you do,' Sheriff George Zimmer concluded.

Deputy Kel Drake returned to the law office just as

35

Sheriff Zimmer downed the rest of his coffee. The puritanical deputy was well into his fifties, lean but lithe. As well as being a lawman he was a Methodist circuit rider, his silver hair trimmed neatly, because he had a weekend's preaching duties coming up and his wife had urged him to look his best. He was known as upright and righteous. Unlike his sheriff boss, he didn't swear, play cards, drink whiskey or mess around with any Lucky Deuce saloon women.

Zimmer wasted no time informing him to keep a close watch on the prisoners until he returned about seven o'clock.

'I sure will, Mr Zimmer,' Drake assured him. 'You can rely on me.'

'I know that, Kel.'

Leaving Deputy Drake in charge, Zimmer saddled his grey gelding and rode swiftly out of town.

He headed straight for his father's Triple Z ranch.

CHAPTER THREE

Luke halted Buck by the picket fence he remembered so well. It had been freshly painted gleaming white, and it fronted a well-tended garden of Indian Mallow, mariposa lilies and a single red rose bush.

Sierra Cooper's four-roomed adobe house in Buffalo Street had originally been built by her grandparents who'd come west well before Brigham Young and his Mormon emigrants explored Utah. When Sierra's folks arrived, there were only Franciscan missionaries, sheepherders and half a dozen drifters in Spanish Wells. Some of those drifters, it was thought, were actually outlaws hiding there from the law.

During the past ten years, all of Sierra's family had died, parents and grandparents, buried four in a row inside the northern fence of the cemetery just in the town limits. Now Sierra was on her own, thirty-two years old, the one and only town school ma'am, unmarried and a prize more than one man in Spanish Wells had desired.

Luke had waited for this moment for four long years. He'd thought about her during the bloody battles of Shiloh and Vicksburg, then Gettysburg later in the war.

During the nights when often the guns fell silent, he'd imagined being with her. He'd thought about them becoming man and wife, sleeping together, bringing up kids. Folks in Spanish Wells had assumed Sierra would become Mrs Dawson because they'd been 'keeping company', but when Luke joined up, they'd agreed to postpone any decision to marry. After all, a man riding to fight the Johnny Rebs might not make it home.

The night before he'd left, she'd promised, 'I'll wait for you.'

Those words still rung in his ears as he walked up the path and knocked on her door. Soft footsteps sounded, then the door opened wide.

Sierra stared at him for a long, incredulous moment before whispering hoarsely, 'Dear God! It's you, Luke!'

She was the same as when they'd parted: slender, wide-eyed, hair tumbling in a black cascade to slim shoulders, beautiful and desirable in a modest blue dress that couldn't conceal her soft curves.

'Been a long time, Sierra,' Luke said, reaching for her.

She came to him immediately, burying her face in his chest as he held her tight.

'Come inside,' she invited, trembling against him.

Luke followed her into the house, closed the door and wrapped both arms around her. After all this time she felt good, oh so good, against him.

Suddenly, however, she backed from his embrace and stood there by the glass-fronted glory box cabinet in her front room, arms folded over her quivering breasts. The instinctive joy at first seeing him was fading from her eyes and now her face turned strangely pale, like pastry.

'Luke,' Sierra said softly. Her voice began breaking. 'I

. . . I hadn't heard . . . from you . . . for two years.'

'Wasn't easy to write,' Luke explained. 'There was a shortage of paper and ink. And the Johnny Rebs often held up stagecoaches carrying mail and burned our letters, just for the heck of it.' Regretfully, he admitted, 'Mind you, our bluecoat soldiers did the same to them. Mostly letters with Rebel stamps on were destroyed.' He heard her sob deeply, but she was still dry-eyed, her back now pressed hard against the wall. He continued, 'Come to think of it, I didn't receive any letters from you for the last half of the war.'

'I . . . hadn't heard . . . so I assumed you were dead,' she blurted out.

Luke grinned. 'Well, Sierra, as you can see, I'm very much alive.'

'Yes, I can see,' she said slowly, her eyes ranging over him like they used to four years ago.

'Honani's safe and well, too,' he told her.

'That's good,' she said tonelessly. 'I'm pleased, very pleased for you both.' She drew in her breath sharply as Luke took two steps towards her. Then she said formally, 'Luke, you shouldn't be here, not alone with me like this.'

'Why not?' he asked.

'It's not fit and proper,' she said, a sharp edge to her voice.

'What's wrong?'

There were tears brimming in her eyes now, tears of regret and sadness but then she pressed her lips firmly together before telling him, 'Luke Dawson, when I didn't hear from you, I feared the worst. You can't blame me for that.' She sobbed, 'I knew I had to put you right out of my mind.'

'Say it straight, Sierra,' he prompted gently.

'I'm about to be married, Luke.' Sierra's words hung in the silence between them. She added softly, 'I'm sorry, I'm so sorry.'

Sierra's announcement hit him like a bullet. He remembered battlefield campfires where pessimistic soldiers had often lamented the probability that their womenfolk wouldn't wait for them. At the time, he hadn't given that possibility any thought. Sierra Cooper had stated she'd be there when he came home and he trusted her.

He felt an icy lump in his chest. He felt a blast of anger that his letters had not been delivered. In one sense he couldn't blame her because she'd thought he was dead, but even so, there was a bitter taste in his mouth knowing now she belonged to another man.

'Who is he?' Luke demanded.

Sierra hesitated before answering, 'Mister Zimmer.'

'Zimmer the sheriff!' he exclaimed incredulously.

'No, not George,' Sierra said hastily. 'I'm marrying his father, Mister Dallas Zimmer. I'm to be a rancher's wife, Luke.' She hesitated before elaborating, 'In less than two weeks from now.' After a long moment, she said, 'While you were away, Mrs Penelope Zimmer died. It was a hunting accident. Her horse reared suddenly and the rifle she held exploded. Bullet ploughed into her breast. They did what they could for her but she died before they could get her to Doc Worthington's surgery. That meant Dallas became a widower . . . again.'

There was silence between them.

Finally, Sierra continued. 'After a while, he began calling on me. I didn't encourage his attentions, Luke, but he was most insistent. At first it was once a week, then

40

almost once a day. He just wouldn't take no for an answer. Then one evening – exactly a month ago, in fact – he asked me to marry him.'

'He's about thirty years older than you, Sierra.'

'I'm aware of that,' she said sharply, looking down at the floor.

'So you're getting hitched to Rancher Zimmer in a few days time?'

'Yes, Luke,' Sierra replied, still averting his eyes.

Turning, Luke said, 'I'll leave you to your preparations.'

'Dallas is a good man, Luke,' she said defensively as he began walking. 'I know he's older than me but as Mrs Zimmer I won't just be the town school-ma'am scraping a living, but a rich cattle baron's wife.'

'Good for you.'

Sierra blurted out, 'Yes, rich, Luke. I'll be someone! I'll live in the finest ranch house in the territory; I'll wear the best clothes money can buy. If Dallas gives me kids, and I'm sure he will, I'll be able to bring them up in luxury.'

'Congratulations,' he said at the gate.

'Luke . . . wait,' she pleaded.

'There's nothing more to say,' he said, untying his bay gelding.

Sierra took half a dozen steps into the garden as Luke swung back into his saddle. She said regretfully, 'I'm sorry I can't invite you to the wedding. Please understand it just wouldn't be appropriate.'

'No, it wouldn't,' he agreed, nudging his horse away from the fence.

He rode away in anger, sheer disbelief and disappointment.

A couple of whiskery old timers he used to know called

41

out to him, welcoming him home, but he didn't hear them. He just rode straight ahead, putting distance between himself and Sierra's house. Like most men on the battlefields, he'd seen death and dying. He'd sometimes felt sick in the pit of his stomach at the sight of mutilated bodies being feasted on by vultures. But what he'd just been told had given him the biggest jolt of all.

He kept riding up the alley to Main Street.

He couldn't feel the throb of his heartbeat. His heart was like a stone and he was cold all over.

Right now he needed a drink.

Reaching Main Street, he saw Honani waiting in the saddle for him outside Fenwick's general store. The Indian had rugs slung over his horse and a sack of flour roped to his saddle horn.

'I'm ready to ride,' the Navajo said.

Luke needed to confide in his Indian friend but that would come later. Instead, he said, 'First, we'll pay a visit to the Lucky Deuce.'

The Navajo raised his eyebrows. 'We?'

Luke declared, 'We've fought together, ridden halfway across America together. Now it's trail's end, so if you're agreeable, we'll have a drink together.' He added, 'I'm paying.'

Honani smiled. 'In that case, I'm agreeable.'

They rode together across the street where they hitched their mounts to the Lucky Deuce's tie-rail.

Luke parted the batwing doors first. The saloon hadn't changed much in four years. Originally a barn, the saloon spanned a whole block between two alleys. A bar counter in need of a paint stretched along the far wall. Two dozen card players and drinkers occupied the tables. Behind the bar was a long mirror and a row of whiskey and brandy bottles on a display shelf. Luke didn't know the man behind the bar counter. Maybe Crawley had retired. After all, he was over eighty when the war started. This new bartender was burly, bearded, with corn-coloured hair flopping over ears that needed a wash. The sign hanging over the bar said his name was Blundell.

Alongside the bar counter were two rooms, Blue Room and Red Room. They both had the same sign on their doors: 'IN USE. DO NOT ENTER.'

Luke headed directly for the bar, with Honani on his heels. It was a relatively quiet saloon, with no one at the piano right now – just quiet conversations between drinkers. A solitary saloon girl giggled as she wriggled on a cowhand's lap. Luke and the Navajo made their way through the tables to where Blundell the bearded bartender, who wore a dirty apron over his check shirt and black pants, glanced up from his copy of the Spanish Wells Clarion.

Eyebrows arching, Blundell looked first at Honani, spat into the sawdust beside his feet behind the counter, then fixed his red eyes on Luke.

Slowly, like a big, lazy bear, he rose from his stool. He kept his eyes on Luke as he said, 'Name your poison.'

'We'll have two beers.'

The bartender frowned. 'So you're going to drink two beers?'

'No,' Luke replied. 'One for me, one for my friend.'

'Your friend's an Injun,' Blundell pointed out.

'You're very observant,' Luke said coldly, fronting the bar.

'Listen, mister, we have a rule in here,' the barman proclaimed. He recited slowly and loudly, 'We don't serve niggers, greasers and Injuns.'

The saloon sounds faded into silence. The girl stopped giggling, poker players looked up from their cards and two tables full of cowhands stopped drinking and yarning.

'Since when?' Luke challenged.

'Listen, stranger—' the bartender said wearily.

'I'm no stranger.'

'Huh?'

'I lived in these parts and drank in this saloon for ten years before I signed on to fight for the Union,' Luke declared.

'OK, OK, soldier-boy, so you're a hero! Keep your shirt on.'

'I'll ask you again and you'll give me a straight answer,' Luke warned. Right now he was in no mood to be trifled with. His tone hardened even more as he repeated, 'Since when?'

The bartender's eyes narrowed. 'Since Mr Dallas Zimmer bought this Lucky Deuce saloon.'

After what Sierra had told him, the very mention of Zimmer made Luke bristle. 'I don't usually ask twice but I'll make an exception in your case,' Luke said, his tone loaded with angry menace. He lifted his six-shooter from its leather and placed the gun on the bar counter. Then he repeated, 'Two beers, bartender. One for me. One for my friend. Pronto!'

The whole saloon froze.

'Listen, mister, even if Mr Zimmer hadn't given his order, I still wouldn't serve a goddamn Injun,' Blundell announced belligerently, his nostrils flaring. 'My family was murdered in their beds by skulking Apaches.'

'Lance Corporal Honani is a Navajo.'

44

The barman sneered, 'I don't give a damn – he's a filthy, stinking Injun.'

'Luke,' Honani counselled quietly beside him, 'forget about the drink. It's not important.'

'I say it is,' Luke disagreed. He spoke loudly now, so the whole saloon could hear. 'This man fought for the Union. He was awarded the Medal of Honour. He deserves a drink and he's going to get one.'

The mirror behind the bar betrayed Blundell's slow, furtive reach for a rifle concealed under the counter. Luke saw Blundell's fat fingers find the metal barrel of the gun neatly concealed between a spare apron and half a dozen glasses. Those fingers crept to the stock and closed around it.

'Go to hell, both of you,' the barman said, lifting the rifle.

Luke Dawson had never contemplated being a professional gunfighter but he could easily have been one because he was no slouch. His right hand swooped like greased lightning to grab the gun he'd laid on the counter.

Even as the bartender's finger found his rifle trigger, Luke aimed and fired. The bullet bored into the bartender's upper left arm, shattering a bone. Howling like a whipped wolf, Blundell dropped his rifle and crashed back against the mirror with blood spilling from his wound. There he stood, fighting the waves of pain swamping his senses.

'Our beers, Blundell,' Luke reminded him quietly.

Swearing, whining, the bartender complied, pulling the drinks and placing them on the bar counter. Then he slumped back on his stool and clamped his right hand over the wound to stem the flow of blood.

45

Luke placed his money on the bar. 'Next time, don't argue.'

They drank together as the saloon slowly returned to normal.

Finally, they strode back outside. Someone had summoned the town medico, and Doc Worthington and his black medical bag came bustling into the saloon to tend the wounded Blundell.

The sun was low in the fading sky and the shadows were lengthening as Luke and Honani rode past Sienna's home, an old dilapidated barn that hadn't been used for years, then Wallace's place where the Confederate flag had just been hoisted on a tall pole and fluttered in the evening breeze.

They reached town limits and took the western trail out of Spanish Wells.

CHAPTER FOUR

Once out of town, Luke and Honani headed between the crumbling granite walls of Sagebrush Pass and then took a wide, wheel-rutted trail that followed the Triple Z fence line. Dallas Zimmer's vast empire of rolling grass slewed away from the fence and then rose slowly again to a long, timbered, windswept ridge that presided over his spread like a regal balcony. Built right under this ridge was a large, imposing stone ranch house that dwarfed a pine-log bunkhouse, three barns and a line of cabins in which the domestic servants slept. Smoke curled languidly from the ranch house's two chimneys into the fading sky.

This was where Sierra would be living soon.

She would be queen of the biggest ranch in Utah, Mr Dallas Zimmer's wife, supervising the cooks and cleaning staff, in charge of entertaining his well-heeled friends – and sleeping in his bed. Her body would be his. But as Zimmer's wife she would be set up for life. Who would blame Sierra for agreeing to marry the rich cattle baron?

Once again Luke felt disappointment mingled with hot anger return to churn him up. The fury would pass in time but right now he was in no mood to be trifled with, as that bartender back in the Lucky Deuce saloon had found out.

Riding together, they saw half a dozen riders drifting amongst hundreds of prime beeves grazing on the lush grass. Every shorthorn was branded Triple Z. They were all in prime condition, some even fat, at least half of them ready to be rounded up for market. Further away from the fence were stockyards full of calves and one corral was packed with spare horses. Seeing this corral reminded Luke again he was riding home to his own Bar LD horse ranch, where wild horses were broken in to be sold in the Spanish Wells stockyards.

He was looking forward to seeing Caleb, his brother, and Caleb's wife Susan. When he'd left them in charge, he promised that on his return the ranch would become a joint venture and they could build their own cabin and live on his land into the future. He'd received no letter from Caleb, but he hadn't expected any. Caleb was no letter writer, and when Luke had left for the war, Susan was hoping for a baby. If kids were tugging at her apron strings, Susan would have had no time to write.

The riders came to a fork in the road.

One trail led north, skirting Zimmer's ranch, leading into mountain country. The other trail twisted around an ancient butte and dropped west towards the big basin the early settlers had named Sundown Valley. It had earned this name when those first pioneers in covered wagons beheld the awesome spectacle of sunset over the valley, when western rims were painted deep crimson and mysterious, darkening shadows crept like giant fingers over the trees and grass. Those early emigrants and their wagons had moved on westwards, leaving the Navajo tribe to live in peace in the valley they'd claimed hundreds of years ago.

Knowing he was close to home, there was jubilation written over Honani's bronze face. He was aching for the first glimpse of his valley. Tonight he would be reunited with his family and sit by the village fire. He would eat and drink with his friends. Out of respect, he would talk long into the night with the tribal elders. He would see the young maidens he'd left behind. He remembered White Lily and the headstrong Runs-Like-Deer.

Then there was Nizhoni, the name meaning 'Beautiful' in the Navajo tongue. Hopefully she would still be available, but maybe, like Luke's woman, she would be taken by now. He would soon find out.

The main thing was that tonight he would sleep in a Navajo lodge. Honani would offer hospitality to Luke, of course, and invite him to stay the night, but he knew what his white friend's answer would be. Like him, after four long years, Luke wanted to get to his log home, which he had raised himself on the tree-clad Old Wolf Ridge that overlooked the valley.

Unable to hold back, Honani urged his shaggy pony past Luke.

The white man was content to keep riding at the same pace and let his Indian friend surge ahead of him. Luke watched the Indian's pony break into an easy lope. He just kept riding, thinking of his brother and his wife, of home cooking and a warm, comfortable bed.

Five minutes later, the Navajo halted his mount on the next crest.

Luke expected to hear a loud whoop of jubilation from his soldier friend, but instead, Honani remained strangely silent. Maybe he was meditating, resting his pony before riding down-slope into the valley of his forefathers.

It was close to sundown and the Navajo rider made a stark, lean silhouette against the blood-red western skies. He was motionless, just sitting saddle, staring down over the valley.

Luke reined his horse alongside his friend and saw why he was frozen to his saddle.

Sundown Valley was in deep shadow but even from this lofty crest, the two riders could make out not just hundreds but thousands of steers below them. They roamed the valley, masses of them, munching on its grass. Their sounds of mooing and bawling drifted up to the crest. In fact, the slight westerly wind even carried their cattle smell to Luke and Honani.

The Navajo raised his eyes to the deep shadows masking the far end of the valley. This was where his village was, although he couldn't see any lodges from this distance. His heart felt like ice. Had some cattleman taken over this valley and left his Navajo people to squeeze into a mere corner?

The herd and the gathering darkness obscured his vision.

All the two riders could see were steers and shadows.

'What has happened to the land of the Navajo?' Honani asked, his tone loaded with trembling anguish and rising trepidation.

'This valley was always open range, regarded for years by all as Navajo country,' Luke said, shaking his head in disbelief at what he was seeing. He frowned as he suggested, without any conviction, 'Maybe your people made a deal with some ranchers?'

Honani replied harshly, 'No! That would not happen! We have remained friends with your people but we would never, never trade our land.' His fury was rising now like a dark tide. 'I will ride down to my village and talk to my people!'

'I'm coming with you.'

'It is not necessary,' the Navajo said.

'We've been together through hell,' Luke reminded him. 'I'm not going to ride out on you now.'

Honani digested Luke's reply for a long moment.

'We ride together,' the Indian conceded gratefully.

They headed down from the crest as the last vivid red glow of sunset showed in the west and the chilly whispering wind rose to meet them. Luke strained his eyes to try and catch a glimpse of the Navajo village, even just a cooking fire, but he saw only darkness. They reached the valley floor and pushed their way between the milling steers. The only brand Luke saw was Triple Z. They pushed further into the herd. Luke looked for other brands but by the time they reached the river that flowed right through the valley, this was the only one he could make out. So far, the cattle baron Dallas Zimmer owned them all.

The riders forded the shallow river, horses' hoofs churning the cold water into white foam, then slashed through tall reeds to mount the far bank.

Again, they were confronted by vast herds of Triple Z cattle.

They kept riding, headed towards the small triangle of land bordered by a winding creek that fed the main river.

It was here, many, many years ago, that the Navajo village had been planted. Yet all Luke and his Indian companion could see was ominous darkness, not even the faintest glimmer of a cooking fire.

They rode in dreadful silence to the creek and reined

their horses on the willow-lined bank. The place where the Navajo village had been for many generations was filled with Zimmer's steers. The two riders saw no Navajos, no hogans, no circles of stones where cooking fires once burned, no mustangs . . . just bare grass and munching beeves.

The sun had settled below the western rims and an eerie full moon was rising as Luke and his Navajo friend splashed across the creek. Luke glanced at Honani. The Indian was thunderstruck, at a loss for words, blood draining from his face as he rode slowly and painfully over the land he still knew like the back of his hand.

Luke watched his Indian friend head his pony right to the cave where the tribal elders used to sit and smoke their pipes. He rode with Honani to the exact place where the big village cooking fire once burned day and night.

The Navajo slid from his saddle, bent down and parted a clump of grass.

The stalks of grass were fresh and green, but when the Navajo pulled some up, the moonlight showed him burned earth. Honani kept walking, his eyes on the ground. He found other black patches, remnants of old Indian fires, then two cooking pots half buried in the clay. He picked up a maiden's necklace, a rusty knife and finally stood where his own dome-roofed hogan had once been. Crouching, the Navajo touched the remains of burnt poles protruding from the soil.

Just then Luke heard the whinny of a horse.

'Honani,' Luke warned sharply. 'We have company.'

Shadowy riders were coming their way, etched like ghosts against the rising moon. Instinctively, Luke rested his hand on the Peacemaker nestling ready in his leather holster as Honani remounted his pony hastily. Luke counted seven riders weaving between the cattle as they approached the willows.

He heard sharp, staccato voices in the night.

'There they are, Mr Zimmer.'

'Over the creek.'

'Yeah, right by that cave.'

'Told you we'd seen 'em.'

Luke saw Dallas Zimmer now, massive and flabby-bellied, astride a snorting black stallion with fire in its eyes. The rancher had always carried too many pounds but he looked almost grotesquely big in the moon glow. What on earth could Sierra see in a man like him? But then, Luke reminded himself bitterly, the cattle baron was rich. That obviously covered a magnitude of sins as far as she was concerned. Luke kept his eyes firmly on Zimmer as the big man urged his horse into the water. He hadn't had much to do with Zimmer in the past, but he recalled one Thanksgiving Day when the arrogant rancher had tried to swindle him in a horse trade. Luke had quoted a price on two mustangs he had for sale, but when he'd delivered the horses Zimmer smugly insisted the deal was for three, 'take it or leave it'. Shrugging, Luke left it, but just as he was about to ride back with the two mustangs, Zimmer relented and sent his ramrod after him. Patrick O'Neill, the dour Irish ramrod, ate humble pie and the deal was done. Luke hadn't forgotten the incident and he was sure Zimmer hadn't either.

The riders forded the creek, hoofs stirring the water into foam. Flanking Zimmer were two men Luke knew. One was the sallow-faced ramrod, O'Neill, riding a chestnut horse. The other was Heck Halliday, who joined the

Union army the same day Luke and Honani signed on. Halliday didn't fight many battles. In fact, like some other soldiers on both sides, he'd deserted after just a month. Luke had often wondered where Halliday had ridden off. Now he knew. The deserter had come back to the Triple Z. There were four other riders, two of them lean Mexicans, the other pair shifty-eyed and unshaven.

All Zimmer's riders were heavily armed. O'Neill wore twin Colt .45s, Deserter Halliday brandished his army rifle, the Mexicans had gloved hands resting on guns and the other two riders had Colts drawn and ready.

'You're trespassing!' Zimmer bellowed.

'Like hell we are,' Luke disagreed, facing the semi-circle of guns. 'This is open range, Navajo land.'

Dallas Zimmer squinted, recognizing him now. Mockingly, the cattle baron greeted, 'Well now, if it ain't our soldier-boy, Luke Dawson, come home from the war.'

'Where are my people?' Honani spoke up loudly.

Irked by the Navajo's urgent question, Zimmer snapped, 'Button your lip. Speak when you're spoken to, Injun!'

'I want to know where my people are,' Honani repeated defiantly.

'And he has a right to ask that question,' Luke said, backing up his Navajo friend.

'An Injun has no rights,' O'Neill guffawed.

'Okay, soldier-boy,' Zimmer said, still ignoring the Navajo. 'You've been away for some time, so it seems you have some catching up to do. This land, Sundown Valley, is no longer open range. As you can see, I'm running my beeves on the grass here and no one's objecting – no one, Dawson. By buying more cattle and having this extra land,

54

I can afford to put on extra hands, thus providing valuable employment opportunities for the right kind of men, some of who are with me right here and now. A fine bunch of boys!' He grinned, showing big, tobacco-stained teeth, with two missing right below his left nostril. 'All hand picked too.'

O'Neill grinned in unison. 'A pleasure to work with them.'

'Where have Lance Corporal Honani's people gone?' Luke demanded.

Halliday raised his bushy eyebrows. 'Lance Corporal, eh!'

'He didn't desert, unlike you,' Luke said.

'It mightn't be healthy to talk like that to my esteemed rider, Mister Heck Halliday,' Zimmer warned him.

'Damnit, where have the Navajos gone?' Luke insisted.

'Who knows?' Zimmer replied, shrugging his flabby shoulders. 'One day they were here, the next day they'd up and gone. Ask my riders. They came to the ranch house and told me.'

'Mr Zimmer's right,' O'Neill said. 'A couple of the boys and me were searching for strays in Sundown Valley. We trailed them to the creek that's just behind us, right to this very spot. We expected to see the Navajos but they simply weren't there. They'd just vamoosed, got up and left everything. We didn't go trailing them; figured it was their business why they'd pulled up stakes and left.'

'My people would never leave their land,' Honani protested emphatically.

'Well, Injun, they did,' O'Neill told him flatly.

'I was one of the riders who discovered they were gone,' Heck Halliday spoke up. 'Damn shame! I had my eyes on

55

one of them Navajo fillies. What was her name now?'

'Fancy name, Flower-of-the-Dawn,' O'Neill said.

'Yeah, that's right.' Halliday grinned lustfully. 'She might have been an Injun squaw but she could have warmed my bed any night!'

Like Zimmer's lawman son and probably others, Heck Halliday regarded Indian girls as being fair game for any white man. As Halliday chuckled, Luke knew that Honani was itching to grab his rifle so he restrained his angry friend with a low-toned warning. 'Hold it! There are seven of them.'

'Fact is,' Zimmer said, 'I instructed my boys to leave the lodges and suchlike in case our Injun friends came back. Then time went by. The Injuns never returned. I figured Sundown Valley was land being wasted so I decided to use it, run some surplus cattle there and give some good, honest white men jobs. Uh, a coupla greasers, too. The Mex boys have been loyal. Might even let them drink in my town saloon one day if they keep up the good work.' The big rancher paused and then said, 'There was no point leaving empty hogans for rats to infest and snakes to crawl into, so I gave the order to burn them.' He smiled, showing his wolfish teeth again. 'Reckon it was the only sensible thing to do.'

'Real sensible, boss,' O'Neill agreed, nodding gravely.

'You burned our homes,' Honani accused hoarsely.

Zimmer leaned forward in his saddle. 'What did you expect us to do? Leave them to rot?'

'Apart from anything else, they were in the way of Mr Zimmer's cattle,' O'Neill concluded.

'Surely someone checked where the Navajos went,' Luke challenged.

'My men had more important chores,' Zimmer shrugged, 'like branding new calves and suchlike. Right, O'Neill?'

'Right, Mr Zimmer,' the ramrod confirmed, nodding.

The Navajo looked around him, eyes brimming with tears.

Luke had never seen him cry, not even when they were confronted with terrible sights of death and mutilation on the battlefield, but the Navajo could hardly hold back right now. This land was part of him. He was part of this land. It was enshrined in his deeply held spiritual beliefs. This was the Indian's worst nightmare. In fact, he'd been cut deep, like a long, sharp knife slashing his flesh.

'My people would never have just got up and left,' the Indian repeated.

'Well, they did,' Zimmer said finally. Dismissing the Navajo, he fixed his eyes on Luke. 'I suppose by now you've heard of my impending wedding to Miss Sierra Cooper. In view of your previous ... uh ... friendship with my bride-to-be, I'm willing to compensate you for your loss. I'm offering you a good well-paid job on my ranch.'

'Not interested, Zimmer,' Luke said bluntly, bristling.

If Zimmer hadn't been backed by six heavily-armed riders, some of whom looked like vultures spoiling for a kill, he'd have been tempted to put a slug in a certain part of the smirking rancher's anatomy that would have sabotaged his wedding night. However, he'd told the Navajo to hold back and he had to do the same himself.

'Think about it,' the cattle baron urged.

'I already have,' Luke said. 'I'm headed for home.'

The rancher declared, 'I realize you're just home from a war so you're not into making big decisions yet. Look,

Dawson, I'll leave the offer open until after my honey-moon.'

'We'll get out of here,' Luke said quietly to Honani.

The Indian took another look at the seven men and their guns and realized, albeit reluctantly, the wisdom of Luke's advice. He asked cautiously, 'But should we turn our backs on them?'

Before Luke could reply to his Navajo friend, Zimmer yelled at him, 'One last thing, Dawson. Don't trespass on my range again. Same goes for the Injun.' But then his tone mellowed. 'Of course, if you join my outfit, you can ride across Sundown Valley any time you like.' He paused before adding, 'Look, I'm a reasonable man, so although I don't usually put Navajos on my payroll, I'm willing to make an exception in your friend's case.' Condescendingly, he said, 'Yep, because he's served in the army, I'll give him a job, despite him being an Injun.'

Honani was shaking with rage, so once again Luke spoke softly under his breath, warning his Navajo friend against making a rash move right now.

'Think about it, both of you!' the cattle baron boomed.

Zimmer turned his big black horse and started back for the creek, followed by O'Neill, then Halliday and the other shadowy riders.

'Like you, I don't trust them, so just ride away slowly, keep your eyes wide open and one hand on a gun,' Luke advised his saddle-pard.

Luke nudged his horse and started riding for the three tall pines that stood in front of the old Navajo elders' cave. Glancing around, he saw the Triple Z riders retreating across the creek. The arrowhead pines blocked out the moonlight, shielding Luke and Honani as they put distance between themselves and the Triple Z men.

Once they reached the cave, Luke halted his horse and looked back. Zimmer's men were lost in the night. Still wary, however, he wasted no time in riding to the ridge trail, finally halting his bay by a clump of sagebrush.

Honani came alongside him, declaring hoarsely, 'I could have killed him.'

'His time is coming but it's not yet,' Luke said.

'My people gone! I cannot believe this has happened!'

'Hard for me to believe, too,' Luke said soberly. 'As long as I've lived on Old Wolf Ridge, I've seen smoke from Navajo fires rising and Navajo hunters coming to and from your village.'

'The elders and the medicine man must have approved leaving the village,' Honani conceded reluctantly, shaking his head in utter despair. 'But why?' Then his eyes narrowed as he suggested darkly, 'Maybe Zimmer and his men lied? They could have come with guns and forced my people to pack up their belongings and leave so they could steal their land.'

'We'll find out,' Luke vowed to his close friend. 'If that actually happened, we'll make Zimmer pay, that's for sure.'

'If they were made to leave, or even if they left peacefully of their own accord, there is only one place where they could possibly be,' Honani decided with his arms folded over his heaving chest. He looked north where moonlight made distant peaks glisten like fresh snow. 'My forefathers belonged to a Navajo clan, the Armijo, who came from Na Dené Canyon. This sacred canyon is beyond the mountains, two, maybe three days' ride from here, on the other side of Whispering Pass, through Apache Territory, under the red butte that towers over all the other canyons. My father twice took me and other young braves there. He used to say Na Dené Canyon was powerful medicine. Perhaps they have returned there?'

'Probably that's what happened,' Luke replied.

'I need to ride to Na Dené Canyon,' the Navajo said firmly.

'Listen, Honani,' Luke said. 'As you know, my spread is an hour's ride from here. You've met my brother Caleb before and he'll be there. It's been a long war and a helluva long trail home. You need to rest and get some shuteye, same as me. You are welcome to have a bed for the night, more if you want.'

Honani considered. 'I will not rest, I will not sleep, until I see my people.'

'Figured you'd say that,' Luke said.

Honani had once told him that Navajos from his clan rarely farewelled friends with 'goodbye.' Rather, it was 'Ya'at'eeh', and the Indian uttered that final word as he made ready to ride.

Luke remembered what that word meant. It was 'see you later'. He hoped this would be so.

The white man responded, 'Yes, see you later, my friend.'

For a long moment Luke Dawson sat saddle, watching as the Indian he'd been with for four years now left him and rode north into the night.

He waited motionless in the saddle until Honani was finally swallowed by the darkness of the distant pine forest.

Sierra Cooper stood perfectly still as her dressmaker, Mrs Lisa Cowan-Jeffries, the local blacksmith's wife, appraised the wedding gown she was making final adjustments to. It was an expensive white dress, conservatively high-necked, flowing in a pure white cascade to her shoes.

Dallas Zimmer, of course, was footing the bill for this dress, Lisa's time and expertise. He wanted to have his new bride looking her best to impress the town of Spanish Wells and he could afford to do so. It would, of course, be Utah's biggest wedding ever, and Cain Zimmer, his dandy brother, was coming all the way from Tombstone City by train, then by stagecoach, for the occasion.

Looking in the long mirror, Sierra knew she looked beautiful and this dress would be perfect for the occasion.

'Are you happy?' Lisa asked suddenly.

Sierra forced a smile. 'Of course. What woman wouldn't be?'

'I was just asking, that's all,' Lisa said quietly.

'You're my dressmaker, and also my friend,' Sierra said. 'If there's something on your mind, say it.'

Lisa bent down and checked the hem. 'My husband Harry was in the Lucky Deuce saloon earlier. He knows I disapprove of alcohol, but he said he'd been working hard and needed a quick drink. Anyway, when he arrived home he told me Luke Dawson's come home from the war. He's alive and well.'

'I'm aware of that, Lisa,' Sierra said sharply.

'Were you two . . . well . . . close?'

'We were friends, good friends,' Sierra replied, fighting back her tears.

The dressmaker murmured, 'I heard you were more than friends.'

'Whoever you've been talking to should mind their own damn business,' Sierra snapped.

Taken aback by Sierra's angry retort, Lisa said, 'Sorry!'

'Whatever Luke Dawson was to me, that was in the past,' Sierra said firmly. Her voice broke. 'In just over a week's . . . time . . . I'll be Mrs Dallas Zimmer.' She swallowed. 'That's all that matters now.'

'Hmm,' Lisa Cowan-Jeffries said under her breath.

'And Lisa, make sure Harry scrubs up and dresses respectable for the wedding,' Sierra warned.

The dressmaker was about to remark that she was sounding like a Zimmer already but she held her tongue. Instead, she maintained near silence as she made a few final alterations to the dress.

Twenty minutes later, Lisa left Sierra and walked the three doors to her modest adobe home next to Major Wallace's place.

Sierra locked her street door and stood there shaking.

Despite all that she'd said to her friend Lisa, she was thinking about Luke Dawson. In fact, she'd had him on her mind ever since she'd opened the door to him earlier today. The way he'd briefly held her, close and intimate, had brought back so many old memories.

Unable to hold back any longer, she wept bitter tears as she stumbled to the solid oak cabinet Zimmer had bought her as an engagement gift. She wrenched open the door and plucked a bottle of brandy from the shelf. Grabbing a glass, she flopped into a cushioned chair and poured herself a drink.

It would be the first of many drinks, tonight and every night between now and the wedding.

CHAPTER FIVE

Luke rode the lonely trail under the rising moon. It was a trail he'd ridden many times in the past and he knew every twist and turn, every fallen tree, every creek that bubbled through boulders and ferns. It was a slow, gradual climb. He heard the hooting of tree owls and the distant baying of wolves from the high country. He passed Lew Harbinger's place, expecting to see lamps glowing and his mangy old dog on the front porch. However, the old trapper's cabin was wreathed in darkness and there was no dog. Maybe Lew was having an early night. Hopefully they'd catch up in a week or so. He drifted by McPherson's cabin. It looked bleak and stark and Luke figured no one had moved in after Clement and Constance had been murdered.

He kept riding.

He was thinking about Honani. By now the Navajo would be heading deeper into the high country, following Muskrat Creek. The thin, little-used track climbed through Whispering Pass, a cleft between the two towering peaks Luke could see glistening in the moonlight through the tall pines. Once through that pass, Honani would make the long journey right down to Na Dené Canyon. The Indian needed answers and Luke knew he wouldn't sleep until he had them.

The trail became steeper suddenly, rising to Old Wolf Ridge.

Luke's bay gelding was tiring, occasionally stumbling. Both horse and rider needed a good night's rest at the Bar LD. In fact, Luke decided that he'd let his horse have a well-earned spell for a month or more. Caleb would have other horses on the spread.

He topped the long rise. Old Wolf Ridge was a large, timbered shelf of clay and rock overlooking Sundown Valley. It stretched west for ten miles, finally dropping to a vast grassy plain that was crossed by the wagon trail used by the early Mormon pioneers. Riding across the ridge, Luke saw the distant lamps of Spanish Wells. They blinked in the night, small pinpricks of light, and even from this distance he knew the one that burned on Sierra's front porch. The memory of their parting was raw, like an open wound as he headed towards his destination. She was a damn fool to be marrying Zimmer but there was nothing he could do about it now.

He saw the Bar LD fence ahead, stretching beyond three towering pines that made arrowheads against the moon.

This was trail's end.

He was home at last!

By now the big weary bay gelding had slowed to a walk, but Luke didn't push him. He let his trusty horse just drift to the fence. He frowned when he saw some strands of wire coiled in the grass and one fence post uprooted. Riding along the fence line he came to the gate that was wide

64

open on rusted hinges. He felt annoyed because he'd trusted Caleb to keep the spread in good order. Luke remembered his brother had been fond of the redeye whiskey and he hoped he hadn't surrendered to alcohol once again. After all, he had a lovely wife and at least one child. Frowning now, Luke told himself Bar LD mustangs could easily escape into the wild through fence gaps and open gates. Just as he rode through onto his land, clouds edged across the face of the moon, affording him only the light from a few stars to see by.

He kept on the track that led from the gate to where he'd built the log cabin overlooking Sundown Valley. He'd sweated chopping down trees and hauling them to the site he'd chosen. One long week of hard work had gone into raising his cabin. Tall stalks of crabgrass weeds were littering the track. He found the bleached skeleton of a horse with foxtail growing between its bones. Growing anger at Caleb's apparent failure to upkeep the fence turned into concern for his brother's well-being as he rode further into the darkness. Caleb's health had never been the best. Maybe he hadn't become drink-sozzled. A decade ago he'd nearly succumbed to a frontier fever. If Caleb had become ill, Susan would never have been able to take care of a horse ranch.

In fact, Luke saw no horses.

He passed the first of their breaking-in corrals. It was empty, more crabgrass forming a tangled carpet over the dusty earth. This corral hadn't been used for well over a year, maybe longer.

Something was wrong, terribly wrong.

Then a shaft of moonlight broke through the clouds and showed him heaps of blackened timber where once his cabin had stood.

For a long moment he simply stared at the crumbled, burned remains of the home he'd built for himself and which Caleb and Susan would have lived in while he was away at the war. He saw slithers of glass, a broken window frame, and a potbelly still standing amidst the ruins. He glanced at where the stables had been built. He saw only charred logs. Luke felt mounting anger. The Bar LD horse ranch that was once a thriving spread had been completely destroyed. Maybe Caleb and Susan had abandoned the cabin and ranch and gone elsewhere. After all, it wasn't exactly an easy life catching and breaking in mustangs and there may have been problems with her baby.

If only his brother had written to him!

But then, moments later, he saw the stones.

They were a few paces from the cabin's charred remains and Luke Dawson's heart was heavy as lead as he dismounted and walked over to them. There were two smooth stones, each planted at the head of some raised earth.

The simple words 'CALEB DAWSON, WITH THE LORD' had been carved crudely on the first one. 'SUSAN DAWSON, HIS WIFE' was the inscription on the second one.

Luke stood like a statue, lean and gaunt, carved against the ghostly moon. It was one helluva homecoming, he told himself.

First he'd learned Sierra was about to marry Zimmer, then he'd shared his Navajo friend's personal disappointment that his people had apparently moved on, and now this shattering discovery of two family graves.

Why hadn't Uriah Kemp, the undertaker, said something

66

to him in Spanish Wells? Or even Sierra? Surely she would have known. He would at least have been prepared for what awaited him on the Bar LD.

Then again, maybe neither of them knew.

Maybe Caleb and Susan had both died of cholera or a fever and were quietly buried by neighbours. That often happened out here on the western frontier. He remembered hearing of outbreaks of black cholera close to here. But what if they'd had a child? There was no smaller stone, no other mound of earth. If a child had been born and likewise succumbed to a fever, maybe whoever buried Caleb and Susan had interred their child with them. Or maybe such a child was still alive, being cared for by neighbours.

There was no way of knowing right now.

He raised his eyes northwards. There was a forest on the other side of the Bar LD fence and he knew two families who lived there, both good neighbours. He could even see a tiny light blinking in the distant darkness. That light was coming from Wishbone Whitehead's place. He needed to pay the old timer a visit. Hopefully he could provide some answers.

Full of bitterness and grief, he remounted Buck and started a lonely ride back across his land. Once on the trail again, he found the track that threaded through the pines towards two cabins, one lived in by Wishbone and his daughter Annie, then deeper into the forest, a second one built by Isaiah and Rose Finlayson. Luke rode that track, forded a murmuring creek and startled a deer that fled into the undergrowth. Finally, he reached the verge of the clearing where Wishbone's log cabin fronted a vegetable garden.

Wishbone's mangy old dog began barking a warning from inside the cabin as Luke headed his horse across the clearing. A single lamp flickered from behind the curtain of Wishbone's parlour window. Even before Luke reached the hitching post by the water trough, the front door eased open to a thin slit and a rifle protruded.

'Freeze, mister, freeze! I mean it, freeze!' It was Annie's voice, high-pitched, trembling, echoing in the night. 'Yeah, stay right where you are, or I'll blast you out of your saddle.'

'Annie,' Luke called to her, halting his horse. 'Annie, it's Luke Dawson.'

The door burst wide open and she stepped outside.

'Well, I'll be doggoned! It sure is!' Annie exclaimed as she lowered her hunting rifle. Her face was glowing as she cried out excitedly, 'Welcome home. Get down from that hoss and come inside, Mr Dawson.'

Annie stood there grinning as Luke eased his tired frame from the bay. The old trapper's daughter wore a deerskin blouse and pants, just like he remembered.

He'd always regarded her as a bit of a tomboy and he'd never seen her in a dress. However, he had to concede, she sure filled out her deerskins to perfection. Now after four years, her hair was much longer, flowing like golden honey to the curve of her breasts. The day before he'd ridden off to war, he'd been invited here for a glass of Wishbone's potent, home-brewed moonshine and he'd remarked then that Annie would surely be hitched by the time he came home. But right now a quick glance told him she wasn't wearing a ring. He looped his horse's reins around Wishbone's tie-rail.

'Is Wishbone awake?'

'Pa will be playing cards with the widow-woman.'

He blinked. 'What widow-woman?'

She replied, 'Widow Rose.'

'You're saying Isaiah Finlayson died?'

'He sure did,' Annie said in a sad tone, ushering him inside. She walked over to the potbelly stove and checked the new coffee pot her father had bought her last Thanksgiving. She'd had it warming on the cooking plate for some time. 'Shooting accident, so folks said, although Rose told us her husband had lived with guns since he was knee-high to a toad. Reckon it happened two years ago, about the same time as—'

'As Caleb and Susan?' he asked quietly.

'Why don't you sit down, Mr Dawson?' Annie invited. 'Please make yourself at home.' When he'd straddled a chair at the table, she asked, 'Could you use some coffee?'

'I sure could,' Luke said. 'However, I'm here looking for answers.'

'Which means you need to talk to my pa,' Annie said hastily, pouring coffee into a large china cup. 'I'll make sure he leaves his card playing, or whatever else he and the widow are up to, and comes a-running.'

She brought his coffee and a plate of home-baked cookies to the table, picked up her rifle and reopened the door. Taking two steps outside into the night, she aimed the rifle at the stars and squeezed the trigger. The explosion ripped the night silence apart and echoed over the forest.

'That'll fetch him,' she said.

Then she stood there waiting as Luke sipped his coffee. Caleb, Susan, the McPhersons and now Isaiah Finlayson had all died since he'd been away. Even now he was wondering about Harbinger, whose derelict cabin he'd passed soon after taking the Old Wolf Ridge trail.

Annie obviously didn't want to say much, preferring to leave it to her father. Luke remembered Wishbone well. After five years stint in jail at the age of eighteen for his part in a bank robbery in Texas, Wishbone latched onto a slim, lively woman who once worked as a saloon whore. Wishbone and Delia rode together to Utah to start a new life. Luke had always given Wishbone credit for this. Once here, on Old Wolf Ridge, Wishbone became a trapper and Delia gave birth to and brought up Annie in this cabin. Sadly, ten years ago when Annie was in her mid teens, Delia was bitten by a fat rattler sunning itself by a nearby creek. Father and daughter did their best to save her but Delia died right here in this cabin and was buried out the back, just past the horse stable.

Luke heard the sound of heavy boots crunching clay.

Moments later Wishbone, puffing and blowing, burst into the clearing.

'Annie! Annie! Are you OK?'

'I'm fine, Pa,' she called out. 'We have a visitor.'

'Visitor! Who in tarnation—'

'Mr Dawson's back.'

'By all that's holy,' Wishbone responded, still running.

Panting, he brushed past his daughter and stumbled inside where Luke had almost finished Annie's coffee. These last four years had not been kind to Wishbone. Unlike his daughter who'd most certainly blossomed, Wishbone had aged considerably since Luke had last set eyes on him. He looked ten years older than his sixty-two years. His hair was white, his beard even whiter and his face was already wrinkled.

70

'Welcome home, soldier-boy,' Wishbone greeted warmly. 'So glad you're back safe and sound.'

The two men shook hands. Luke noticed that Wishbone's right hand had its thumb missing and his grip wasn't as firm as he once knew it to be. The old woodsman was still panting too, wheezing loudly. When he'd heard the gunshot, which he'd known would have come from their cabin, he'd thought the worst and belted out of the widow's cabin to get here as soon as he could. He was relieved all was well but he knew immediately what would be on Luke Dawson's mind.

'Reckon you've been to your place.'

'What happened to my kin, Wishbone?'

Wishbone slumped into his chair. 'Coffee for me too, Annie.'

'Sure, Pa.'

Luke waited but Wishbone said nothing more until he had a few quick sips of his daughter's coffee.

'We were away when it happened,' Wishbone said, shaking his head. 'There was a gold strike south of here, just over Pioneer River. Nuggets as big as a man's fist, so the stories went. Because you were away fighting those Johnny Rebs, you wouldn't have heard of it.'

'I heard nothing.'

'I pulled up stakes and Annie came along with me,' Wishbone recalled. 'We registered a claim, panned for gold in the river, same as hundreds of others, but all we found were a couple of real small gritty pieces we were paid seven lousy bucks for. After that, we rode home so I could take up trapping again.' He added, 'That's when we saw them.'

'We thought to pay our respects to Caleb and Susan so

71

we went calling,' Annie said miserably.

'We found the charred remains of the cabin and two fresh graves,' Wishbone told him in a grim tone. 'It didn't seem right to dig them up to check who they were, but when we rode to Spanish Wells to stock up supplies, our worst fears were confirmed. I paid a visit to the Lucky Deuce and heard the saloon talk. Apparently, your brother Caleb was hanged.'

'Hanged!' Luke echoed. 'What the hell for?'

'According to Blundell the bartender and others, Caleb was strung up for rustling some of Dallas Zimmer's steers.'

'My brother would never—'

'I'm not saying I believe it, I'm just saying what was told to me,' Wishbone said hastily. 'Saloon talk said Caleb was seen cutting out half a dozen Triple Z steers and driving them to your Bar LD spread. Zimmer and a bunch of his men rode up to Old Wolf Ridge and found them. It was like Caleb was caught red-handed. They hanged him from that big arrowhead pine that's right on the edge of your spread, overlooking Sundown Valley. I checked the rope marks on the lowest branch. He was hanged there sure enough.'

'Hanged . . . without a trial?'

'It was a necktie party, plain and simple.'

'Bastards!' Luke said hoarsely.

'Yeah, bastards,' Wishbone agreed.

'Susan?'

Wishbone was melancholy now. 'Blundell told me he heard that while they were dragging her man from their cabin, Susan came at them with a rifle. At long last, after lots of trying, she was pregnant.'

'Then one of them shot her dead, Mr Dawson,' Annie

repeated what her father had told her. 'Yes, he killed a woman about to give birth.'

'It was Heck Halliday,' Wishbone recalled.

'That goddamn deserter,' Luke said slowly, brimming with fury.

'Halliday must have killed Susan right before Caleb's eyes,' Wishbone said, shaking his head. 'Then they executed him.'

'They'll pay, every last one of them,' Luke vowed. His face was ashen, drained of blood as he thought about Caleb dancing rope with his heavily pregnant wife dead on the ground.

Wishbone shrugged. 'Blundell told me they shovelled clay over Caleb and Susan. When I rode over again, I used my hunting knife to carve their names on two pieces of rock. Figured it was the decent thing to do.'

'I'm beholden to you, Wishbone,' Luke said sincerely.

'I . . . I just regret I was so far away when it happened,' Wishbone said, downcast. 'If I'd been around, I'd have stood up for Caleb.'

'Don't blame yourself, Wishbone,' Luke said quietly. 'I was away too.'

Luke had never been a man who harboured hate. Even during the bloodiest battles of the civil war he actually hadn't hated the enemy. Sure, he'd despised a bunch of Southern soldiers for their brutal slaying of a couple of prisoners who'd attempted to escape, but he hadn't actually hated them for their crime. But right now, having heard his brother Caleb was hanged and his wife shot down like a dog, he couldn't help the hate smouldering inside him for the perpetrators.

'What happened to the Navajos?' Luke demanded.

Wishbone drank more of his coffee. 'All we know is that when we arrived back from Pioneer River, they weren't here. Folks said they must have just abandoned their village and left.'

'Maybe Lew Harbinger knows what happened,' Luke said as Annie refilled his coffee mug.

'Maybe he does, but he ain't around to answer any questions,' Wishbone Whitehead said. 'You see, Lew's in Glory Land, another one who died while we were away. His sister Venetta found him dead on his cabin floor when she came visiting. Must have been there for a while because he stank to high heaven. There was no way of telling how he died, Venetta said. She dug a grave out back, read a few verses from the Good Book and buried him. There's a little wooden cross to mark the place. I must remember to carve his name on it when I'm passing next time.'

Luke thought about the desolate, silent cabin he'd passed on his way up here. Harbinger's place had been raised directly over the Indian village and the old man had often traded with them. There was talk he'd even considered taking an old Navajo widow squaw as his wife. Luke remembered her. She was an elderly but sprightly basket-weaver with greying hair.

Old Wolf Ridge had become a rim of death.

Harbinger, Caleb, Susan and Isaiah Finlayson, all dead, the Navajos moved on, all probably within days of each other. Too much of a coincidence, Luke told himself grimly. The dark, murky hand of suspicion shrouded every death on Old Wolf Ridge. And Luke Dawson vowed he wasn't going to merely resume living as if nothing had happened. He had no home, no horses to break in, so he'd be

74

poking around as soon as it was daylight.

'Sorry you came back to this,' Wishbone said despondently. He observed, 'You look damn tired, Luke. Stay here tonight.'

Luke thought about it. 'That's real neighbourly of you. I might just take up your offer.'

Wishbone caught his daughter's smile and noticed the speculative way Annie was glancing at the man who'd come home from the war. There was a certain look in her eyes, one he hadn't noticed before. It was the kind of look a woman gives a man she's attracted to. Wishbone reminded himself that she'd led a sheltered life up here in the forest. Maybe too sheltered.

'I told Widow Rose I'd be back, as usual, but . . . uh . . . I'll stay here tonight,' Wishbone decided hastily, ignoring his daughter's frown.

In less than an hour Wishbone was snoring in his room, Annie curled up awake in hers, with Luke Dawson not sleeping but resting on the spare bunk close by the warmth of the potbelly.

Honani sat hunched over the small fire he'd lit an hour ago, just before midnight. He'd followed the old creek trail since leaving Luke, riding beside running water that bubbled and gleamed under the rising full moon. Finally, however, his pony needed a spell, so he made camp here under a silver spruce.

Yellowy flames licked small logs in a circle of stones. Right now he didn't feel like eating, not even the hardtack he had, but tomorrow he'd shoot a deer.

Looking into the dancing flames, Honani wrestled with what had happened. Why had his father and the other

75

Navajos left the village they'd lived in for centuries? Had the elders, whom he'd not always agreed with, decreed the tribe should return to the ancient home of their Armijo clan in the sacred Na Dené Canyon?

But why? Had they been forced to leave by Zimmer? Surely the young braves would have put up a fight! If there had been a full-scale land war between the Navajos and the Triple Z, someone would have told them when they passed through Spanish Wells.

Or maybe not? Many white men cared little or anything at all about the Indians. Luke Dawson, of course, had been an exception, but then he was like a brother.

Honani told himself that the answers he sought would surely be found in Na Dené Canyon. He recalled in the night silence how many other Navajo braves had regarded him as somewhat of an outcast for leaving his tribe to fight in a white men's war. All except his younger brother, who'd wanted to ride with him. His father, Nastas, however, had forbidden the sixteen-year-old Shiye to leave. Yes, Honani had many questions to ask his family, but above all, he longed to meet them once again.

The Navajo was right on the creek bank so he leaned over to scoop water from the creek. When he did so, the Medal of Honour he wore around his neck glinted in the moonlight. He was certainly proud of receiving the medal, but now that achievement was fading fast in the light of coming home to white men's steers grazing where once his people had lived.

The fire glow played over his bronze face as he reached over to place the coffee pot in the embers.

Right then he heard the distant howling of wolves. It was a big pack, a very big one.

76

Suddenly, the howling stopped. All was silent.

Instinctively, the Navajo's fingers closed around his army rifle.

CHAPTER SIX

Lying awake on his bunk, Luke Dawson heard six shots. They came from a long distance away but they were clear as church bells, four together, the last two a few seconds later. Luke rose swiftly to his feet, opened the cabin door, stepped outside and listened as the echoes faded slowly into the starlit night.

Clad in his tattered old shirt, grubby long-johns, socks full of holes and fur hat, Wishbone shuffled from his room with the last inch of a red-tipped cigarette drooping from his lips. Muttering, he joined Luke at the door.

'Reckon they came from Whispering Pass,' Luke judged.

'Figured that too,' the old trapper confirmed. He thought about it. 'It's a bit late for a hunter to go shooting deer, but he might fire bullets to scare off a pack of hungry wolves sneaking too close to his campfire.' He recalled, 'That's happened to me a couple of times.'

'The creek trail goes through the pass,' Luke reminded him.

'Now I know what you're thinking, Luke,' Wishbone said, flicking ash from his cigarette. He elaborated, 'Your

Navajo pard took that trail.'

'He sure did, Wishbone.'

The trapper consulted his old wooden wall clock. Sometimes it worked, sometimes it didn't, but now it showed ten minutes to one. He calculated, 'First light's six hours away.'

'I'm not waiting for first light.'

Wishbone protested, 'Goddamnit, Luke! You can't go scoutin' around in the dark!'

'I'll latch on to the creek trail and follow it up into the pass,' Luke told him. 'Hopefully I'll just find a few dead wolves.'

'And that's probably all you will find,' Wishbone snorted.

'But I'm riding, all the same.'

'You're stubborn as a flaming mule, Luke Dawson,' Wishbone muttered. 'However, if you're intent on taking a ride, use one of my hosses. Your bay looked deadbeat, so saddle up my big chestnut. He's yours for as long as you need him. Name's Red Jack, stabled next to Annie's mare. Mind you, he won't appreciate being taken out of the stable at this hour, but being a hoss wrangler you'll soon show him who's boss.'

'Thanks, Wishbone.'

'Look, I'll ride with you,' Wishbone decided to volunteer.

'Your place is home with your daughter.'

'Annie can keep Widow Rose company,' Wishbone said. He stubbed his cigarette on the potbelly's top. 'Give me one minute. I'll get into my trapper's clothes, fetch my gun and be with you.'

Luke wasn't going to argue with him. Besides, he'd been

79

away for four years and old Wishbone would surely know any new shortcuts to the creek.

'I'll saddle your chestnut,' Luke said, leaving Wishbone to stumble back to his bedroom to put on some clothes.

Luke was about to leave for the stable when Annie's bedroom door opened and she stood there holding a flickering oil lamp. Awakened by the sounds of talking, she too had scrambled out of bed and hastily donned her long brown dressing gown.

'What's going on, Mr Dawson?' Annie asked.

Luke reached for his rifle. 'Taking a ride, Annie.'

'Right now?' she exclaimed.

'Heard some shots,' Luke said. 'Probably nothing to worry about, Annie, but as a precaution, Wishbone and me aim to do some checking. Meantime we'll take you to Widow Rose's place.'

'I'm perfectly capable of staying here and looking after myself, Mr Dawson,' Annie blazed indignantly.

'I'm sure you are, Annie,' Luke agreed wryly, 'but look at it this way. The widow-woman, Mrs Finlayson, will surely feel safer if you're there keeping her company.'

Annie thought about it for a moment. 'Well, if you put it that way. . . .'

Leaving her, he strode to the stable behind Wishbone's cabin and proceeded to saddle Red Jack. It wasn't long before he heard a footfall behind him. Annie arrived holding up the lamp for him so he could see better. The lamp's glow framed her too and Luke couldn't help but notice the way her woolly dressing gown clung deliciously to her shapely figure. For the second time since arriving here, Luke told himself she was no longer the tomboy he used to know. Again he wondered why she didn't have a man. As he was thinking this, Wishbone hobbled into the stable and threw his saddle over a sleepy-looking piebald. Meanwhile, Annie ran to her room and shrugged into her deerskin pants and top.

With two horses saddled, Wishbone told his daughter to climb up behind him so they could take her to the widow's cabin.

'Two of us would be too heavy for Baldy,' Annie protested. 'How about I ride with Mr Dawson? Red Jack's so strong he'd take three riders.'

Before Wishbone could argue, she balanced on a stall rail, mounted up behind Luke and wrapped her arms around his chest. She fitted against him perfectly. He felt her heart beat against his back as they rode up the track to Widow Rose's cabin.

While Annie dismounted, Wishbone hastily explained to the widow why they were here.

'Ride careful, Pa,' Annie said as Widow Rose prepared to usher her inside. She smiled up at the Union soldier. 'You too, Mr Dawson.'

He grinned. 'No need to call me Mr Dawson. The name's Luke.'

'Keep safe, Luke,' she said softly.

Luke and Wishbone rode away from the cabin.

He knew Wishbone thought he was crazy investigating half a dozen gunshots after midnight. After all, there were trappers and hunters throughout the high country, many of them resting up in night camps where savage wolves could be a problem. It was highly likely one of them had fired a barrage of shots at the scavengers. All the same, Honani was up there somewhere and the loyalty forged in many battles meant he had to take this ride to Whispering

Pass. Unless Honani had already ridden right through the pass and was too far away, in all probability they'd meet up with him, share hot coffee by his campfire and then go their separate ways.

At least he'd ride back with peace of mind.

True to Wishbone's prediction, the chestnut did not take kindly to being ridden by a stranger, especially at night, but Luke's firm handling and reassuring talk settled the horse. Although this was country he knew well, he was glad Wishbone had insisted on riding with him. The old trapper pointed out a thin, winding track he'd forged while Luke was away fighting in the war. Instead of having to reach the creek first, Wishbone's new trail climbed directly north and then ran across the timbered rim that jutted out a mile below Whispering Pass. A quick ride along this rim brought them to the familiar creek trail Luke knew well. It had saved them an hour's ride.

The tall pines tended to block out the moon and many stars as they rode towards the towering cleft between two mountains. After a while, they came upon a clearing where they were able to read recent hoof prints left in the clay. They'd been made by a smaller horse, maybe a pony. Maybe Honani's brown pony. Then, a mile later, Luke saw other hoof marks made by more than one horse. These prints were very fresh, made just a couple of hours ago.

Following the trail, Luke and the trapper rode swiftly across a timbered, fern-clad flat, rounded three bald boulders and reached the big, yawning mouth of Whispering Pass. Here the creek ran faster, racing over stones, bending the reeds. They rode their mounts into the pass. The eerie howling of wolves came to them.

Following the creek now, Luke rode in front, Wishbone

just behind him. The stark granite walls of Whispering Pass rose high on both sides and the riders felt the cold eerie wind that gave the pass its name.

The trail twisted and turned with the creek. The night grew darker as the overhanging walls of the pass blocked out more stars. Luke glimpsed white eyes and furtive shapes slinking in the darkness. He heard the snap of twigs and the crackle of dry leaves being trodden by padding feet.

Luke and Wishbone were now both being brushed by arrowhead pine branches as they mounted deeper into the pass.

They heard the ghostly howling of a nearby wolf pack in the night. Minutes later, Luke smelled smoke. Then they both glimpsed a small ruddy glow through the timber.

They urged their horses between two spruce trees and saw over a dozen wolves circling a campfire. The hungry grey predators were yelping, snarling and snapping as the riders burst through the undergrowth. Riding hard just ahead of the trapper, Luke fired a single shot that felled a grey wolf. Immediately the pack fled for the pines.

Coming closer, Luke smelled burning flesh. He made out the dark shape of a man sprawled across the smouldering remains of a cooking fire. Blackened tatters of material were fluttering amidst the smoke. Flames were still licking the blood-soaked body, roasting him.

Overcome by cold, terrible dread, Luke Dawson rode across the clearing. Still holding his rifle, he slid from his saddle and with one hand hauled the body off the burning coals. For a long moment he simply crouched there, staring in sheer horror at the charred corpse.

Wishbone emptied his saddle, retched violently and

stood back.

'My God! Honani!' Luke cried hoarsely.

'Hell's bells,' the trapper croaked.

There were two holes in the base of the dead man's scorched neck and another four scattered either side of his spine, accounting for the number of shots Luke had heard echoing in the night.

'All six in the back,' Luke said tonelessly. 'Whoever did this must have snuck up on him.'

'Yellow bastards,' Wishbone spat out.

Luke turned the body over.

Honani's face was hideously swollen and scarlet, his eyes mere hollow sockets. His lips were burnt to ashes. Part of his cheek had been burned right through to the bone. He'd known soldiers to weep when their friends were killed in battle but right now he held back the tears that could so easily flow.

Instead, he was consumed with terrible rage as he made a silent vow: whomever did this would rot in Boot Hill.

His eyes drifted over the Navajo's body again. There was no hair on the crown of his head, not even a few lingering strands, and he noticed a deep groove across the top of his forehead. Wishbone saw what he was looking at.

'He's been scalped,' the trapper wheezed.

'Looks like it.'

'Filthy Apaches!' Wishbone spat.

Luke scouted around. The Navajo's pony, saddle and bedroll were gone. His food pack, tin wallet and rain slicker were nowhere to be seen. His guns had been taken. His killers, whoever they were, had taken all his worldly possessions. Luke assumed there was more than one killer because the clay around the dying fire had been churned over by many feet.

'They cleaned him out,' Luke Dawson said. 'Stole every-thing, even his Medal of Honour.'

'Probably hanging in an Apache wickiup,' Wishbone remarked.

'Maybe,' Luke said.

Wishbone needed a cigarette right now so his shaking fingers built one while Luke walked around the clearing. Luke halted, finding spent shells scattered on the far side of a fallen log. This was where the lethal shots had been fired. Scouting around, he saw hoof prints clearly defined in the soft black clay. He struck a match for light and exam-ined them closely.

'It wasn't Apaches,' Luke said.

'But he was scalped—'

'Fact is the murdering back-shooting swine were three, maybe four white men,' Luke announced from the edge of the clearing. He explained, 'Apaches ride unshod ponies. The horses ridden by these lowdown cowards were shod at a blacksmith's forge.'

'So what are you saying?'

'The sidewinders who killed Honani were as white as you and me,' Luke said bluntly. 'My friend was deliberately scalped to make it look like Apaches were responsible.'

Wishbone frowned. 'But why?'

'That I intend to find out.'

Puffing on his cigarette, Wishbone stood over the Navajo. Their trails had crossed more than once and they'd traded in the village that used to be in Sundown Valley. No man should die like this. No man should go to his grave looking so grotesque as this. He retched again and finally threw up.

'Wishbone,' Luke said quietly, beside him now. 'I need a favour.'

'Name it, Luke.'

'My Navajo friend deserves a decent, safe burial place and that's not here in the wilderness. Those wolves are watching us from the darkness. If we bury him here, once we leave they'll be back to try to dig him up. I'm asking you to take him back and bury him deep on my Bar LD land. Meanwhile, I have business to attend to. I don't need to tell you what I have in mind.'

Wishbone shook his head. 'Luke, Honani wouldn't want you to get yourself killed on his account.'

'I'll wait here till first light and latch on to their trail,' Luke told him.

'Even if you manage to track them down, there are three or four of them,' Wishbone protested, recalling what Luke had said. He warned, 'You can't take on that number!'

'I can try.'

Luke helped Wishbone rope the Navajo's burned body to his horse. The trapper hauled himself back into the saddle and picked up his reins.

'I'll bring Red Jack back as soon as I can,' Luke told him. 'If I don't make it, my bay horse is yours.'

Wishbone rode into the night.

Luke stood by the dying fire.

He had three hours to wait before dawn.

Thinking about his soldier friend, Luke stared into the flames that became glowing embers and wisps of smoke.

He spent a long, lonely vigil remembering his loyal friend, thinking of when they'd fought side by side, reliving the many times they'd faced the enemy together in the searing heat of summer and the icy cold of winter. He swallowed deeply, recalling that proud moment when he'd watched Lance Corporal Honani receive the nation's highest military honour. There was no way he'd let those murdering thieves get away with stealing that medal!

He reflected that they'd both ridden home together from the war, each man yearning for peace and a good life. Within hours of their return, Honani had been murdered, ruthlessly shot in the back.

They'd both returned to greed and death.

And Luke Dawson was now a hunter ready to kill.

CHAPTER SEVEN

It was first light.

The smudge of grey over the far eastern rim of Whispering Pass turned into blazing gold as Luke Dawson followed the hoof prints to the creek bank. There he mounted Red Jack and rode through the freezing water to the bed of reeds on the other side. He saw where horses had ploughed a path through the tall, stalky reeds to a ferny flat. Here snapped ferns and hoof marks in the clay clearly showed him the killers' trail.

Halting the chestnut, he took a close look at the tracks in the new light flooding into the pass. There were five sets of hoof prints. One would belong to the Navajo's pony, which meant there were definitely four riders he was trailing. By now they were six hours ahead of him.

The tracks followed the creek out of the pass, then headed northeast across two wide flats. Luke was glad they were well ahead of him right now because any man with a rifle on the far side of a flat could pick him off easily as he rode the open space. Deer watched him from a distance and a lone buzzard circled overhead as he finished crossing the flats. The trail was fresh, easy to read through this high country wilderness.

It was mid-morning when he came upon the hollow where the murderers had stopped to rest their horses. Cigarette butts littered the flattened wild rye grass and tiny wisps of smoke curled like worms from a small black circle in the earth, betraying where they'd lit a fire to boil coffee.

Luke pushed ahead, tracking the hoof prints down from the mountains. He forded a lazy river and then rode through a silent, low-walled pass. Here the clay became harder, making the hoof marks less pronounced, slowing him down. Once he even lost the trail, meaning he had to scout around until he found the tracks once more. He told himself that Honani would have picked them up in half the time. High noon passed. Four hours later the shadows began to lengthen as the trail forked south towards a shallow valley.

He saw more cigarette butts and deeper hoof marks in mud where they'd rested their horses again by a waterhole.

Luke kept riding, threading his way through sagebrush and bald boulders right to the rim of the valley. That's when he saw the smoke curling languidly into the dusky sky.

He halted Red Jack and looked across the valley below. The smoke was coming from a fire burning out the front of a crude cabin that had been built between two arrow-head pines. The back wall of this stone cabin was wedged into the crumbling granite slope that hemmed in the far side of the valley. The hoof prints he'd been following led down a steep slope to the valley floor. They looked to be headed straight in the direction of the cabin.

But it was all open country. If the killers were holed up in that cabin, they'd see him coming. In fact, if he stayed here on the rim of this valley wall much longer there was a good chance they'd spot him anyway, so he backed Red Jack away from the crest and swigged water from his canteen. He thought about circling the valley, hoping to find a cleft in the rock to ride through, but instead he decided to wait here till sundown.

Luke checked each of his guns, making sure they were all loaded and ready to kill as the sun drifted to far western rims. Dusk enfolded the land like a grey burial shroud. The shadows grew deeper, stretching longer.

The fire lit out the front of the cabin began to glow in the gathering darkness.

It was time.

Luke remounted Red Jack and rode the chestnut back to the valley rim. Holding his rifle, he headed down the slope. He rode slowly and silently to the valley floor. Even in the half-light, he could still make out the killers' tracks plainly. They speared straight across the valley to the cabin but instead of following them directly, Luke urged the chestnut to the southern slope and began to circle.

By now the sun had set. The valley was wreathed in darkness but the distant fire drew him like a beacon. A cold night wind blew down from the mountains and raised puffs of dust as he loomed closer. He heard voices, then ribald laughter. Keeping to the darkest shadows, Luke rode slowly and carefully, keeping a tight rein on Red Jack, guiding the chestnut right to the very edge of the firelight. There he slid noiselessly from his saddle. He crept to a smooth boulder where he crouched low.

Two men stood by the fire. He knew them straight away. They were Abe Thompson and Sam West, the two outlaws who'd held up the Wells Fargo stage. The tallest one,

Thompson, was chewing away at a handful of deer steak while his companion, the lean and rakish West, was closer to the fire, warming his hands. Luke stared incredulously at them from the darkness. He'd left them both locked away in the Spanish Wells jail, so what in hell were they doing here? Had they escaped? Were they busted out? Maybe a smart, slick-talking lawyer had persuaded a judge to release them? Or was there another reason they were no longer behind bars? These men were robbers and killers. If anything, they should be dancing rope, not out here free.

Right then the burly figure of a man waddled out of the cabin. Built like a bear, he was heavily bearded with a crimson scar bulging under his left eye. Luke knew him immediately. He was William 'Bill' Scurlock, whose reward notice he'd seen still displayed prominently just outside the Spanish Wells law office. He looked ten years older than his poster picture. Bill Scurlock had always been a loner but things had obviously changed while Luke was away. By the way Scurlock was bellowing orders at the other two men, he was now boss of this outlaw outfit. Thompson and West rode for him and this must be their hideout. They were obviously the bunch who'd murdered Honani. But he'd trailed four riders here. Where was the other one?

Staked out behind the boulder, Luke kept his eyes peeled. His trigger finger was itching but he didn't want to start shooting and have the fourth killer sneak up on him. So he waited behind his rifle. He smelled the stench of their whiskey. He saw Thompson light a fat cigar. Scurlock produced a pack of cards and West gulped down more redeye.

It was fully dark now. Clouds just began to edge tentatively across the face of the moon. He heard the barking of distant coyotes.

Luke's patience was wearing thin. Maybe the fourth killer had ridden out. It was then Thompson bent over to light a second cigar in the glowing coals of their fire. Fleetingly an object hanging over the front of the outlaw's shirt glinted in the firelight. It was the Navajo's Medal of Honour.

Immediate fury welled up inside Luke Dawson. Throwing all caution to the winds, not caring that there could be more outlaws here, he aimed square at Thompson's chest and pulled his trigger. The rifle bullet blasted straight through Abe Thompson's heart, lifting him clean off his feet and then toppling him like a felled log.

Scurlock and West slapped leather as Luke fired again, this time hitting the bearded outlaw high in the right shoulder. Scurlock's outburst of profanity rang out over the valley as he emptied his own Colt revolver at the avenging shadow in the night. Bullets chipped splinters of rock from Luke's boulder, one ripped past his face so close he felt its searing hot breath. Relentlessly, Luke kept firing till his third bullet bored a smoking hole between Scurlock's eyes, killing him where he stood.

Meanwhile West ran for his tethered horse. Frantic, the fleeing outlaw grabbed his saddle and threw it over his grey gelding as Luke left the shelter of his boulder and started walking towards him, emptying his rifle. Bullets thudded into the dust at West's feet. Panic-stricken, the grey gelding reared and West turned to face Luke who'd now lifted his Peacemaker from its holster. Two guns blazed together but the lunging horse struck West, knocking him off balance, spoiling his aim. West's bullet winged high into the stars but Luke's shot burned deep into the outlaw's chest. He sank to his knees and pitched forward, crashing lifelessly into the dust.

Luke stood over Thompson's body. The Navajo's Medal of Honour was resting on Thompson's bleeding chest, secured by a leather cord around his neck. Enraged, Luke stooped down and carefully pulled the looped cord over Thompson's head and dropped the medal into his shirt pocket. It was then he counted the horses tied to a long rail. Apart from Honani's pony, there were four horses, meaning the one last outlaw was possibly still here.

Luke headed slowly towards the open door of the stone cabin. Bursting inside, he saw a single candle burning beside a half-full whiskey bottle. But there was no one in the cabin.

Once outside, he began to walk back to where Red Jack was waiting. He couldn't see the shadow concealed in a small hole of a cave in the valley wall alongside the cabin. This shadow held a long Henry Lever rifle and it was aimed square at Luke Dawson's back as he reached his chestnut horse.

Just as Luke climbed back into the saddle, the rifle thundered from the cave, smashing into his right shoulder. Luke sank over Red Jack's head. He dropped his gun as pain raced through him like a dark, evil tide.

Fighting to keep his balance, Luke just managed to catch a glimpse of the man who'd shot him. He was Heck Halliday, the cowardly deserter who rode for Dallas Zimmer, the ruthless Triple Z rider who'd shot Caleb's wife dead, killing not only her but her unborn child.

Luke swayed in his saddle, then tumbled to the ground. He groped for his fallen Peacemaker but it was too far away, somewhere in the darkness. If only Halliday knew it, Luke was at his mercy. But Heck Halliday wasn't hanging around. In fact, he scrambled out of the cave, hardly affording Luke's sprawled body a second glance as he loped for his mount.

While Luke lay on the ground fighting to stay conscious, the deserter saddled his horse, left the camp and rode furiously into the night.

The bullet burned like a fiery furnace in Luke's back. Blood soaked his shirt, pain knifed up and down his spine, his fingers dug into the earth, and finally he drifted into a darkness that was darker than the night itself.

It was midnight but lamps still lit up the Triple Z ranch house as Heck Halliday rode in from the range. Approaching, Halliday heard the sound of music and approaching closer, he saw folks talking and drinking on the front porch. He recognized the town mayor, Preacher Thomas Grayling, Doctor Worthington and his vivacious wife, all with wine glasses in their hands.

The negro servant, Elijah, was singing 'Nelly Bly' to the accompaniment of piano and banjo. Dallas Zimmer himself, impeccably dressed in a pinstriped black suit, starched shirt and necktie, was hovering over his betrothed, Sierra Cooper, resplendent in a long black gown. As he rode in, Halliday told himself that his boss had chosen a real fine filly to be his third wife. His first wife, Grace, had died of a frontier fever when she was quite young and Penelope, his second, was buried last year. From what he'd seen of Sierra, the new Mrs Zimmer would fit in well with life on the Triple Z.

Tonight Zimmer was holding a pre-wedding party,

exactly one week out from the actual ceremony. Heck Halliday reminded himself he needed a visit to barber Sam Garner before the wedding.

He rode into the dancing light thrown by a dozen lanterns hanging in a long row under the verandah roof. Elijah had just finished his song and was bowing to the mild applause. Rancher Zimmer saw Heck Halliday immediately and nodded to his ramrod, O'Neill. Leaving his fiancée Sierra to talk to the mayor's wife, Zimmer joined O'Neill in the front garden and together they trampled a bed of flowers as they strode to the incoming rider.

'What took you so long?' Zimmer demanded harshly.

'We trailed the Injun, like you told us to, and filled the varmint with lead,' Halliday boasted, still in the saddle. He chuckled, 'He certainly won't cause you any trouble now. He's in the Happy Hunting Grounds.' Then he added, 'I figured it wouldn't do any harm to have a few drinks with our outlaw friends back in Bill Scurlock's cabin before coming here, but it seems Dawson latched onto our trail.'

'Dawson!' Zimmer exclaimed. He growled, 'Hell, I knew it was a mistake not to kill him when he trespassed on our land in Sundown Valley!'

'He must have found the Injun's body and trailed us,' Heck Halliday told them. 'He arrived at Scurlock's camp and started shooting like a crazy man.'

'Keep your goddamn voice down,' Zimmer growled a warning.

Halliday continued, quieter now. 'Dawson killed the whole gang, Scurlock, West and Thompson. Wiped them all out.'

'So how come you're still breathing?' O'Neill wanted to know.

'I was in that cave behind their cabin,' Heck Halliday said. He added hastily, 'I wasn't there because I was spooked. . . .'

Zimmer's eyebrows arched. The rancher knew full well that he had a deserter on his payroll. Although Zimmer had been pleased enough to welcome the Union trooper back into the fold, he always considered that men like Halliday could turn yellow in certain circumstances.

'So why were you there?' the rancher asked, glancing back over his shoulder to make sure none of his guests were close enough to hear.

'Thompson told me they kept their outlaw loot in that cave,' Halliday explained. 'Figured on helping myself to a bagful, then Dawson rode up.'

'So you hid there until he left?' O'Neill sneered.

'No, I killed him,' Halliday said proudly.

'Maybe we've been wrong about you, Heck,' Zimmer said, grinning.

'Yeah, I reckon so,' Ramrod O'Neill agreed.

Halliday boasted, 'One bullet was all I needed. Blasted him clean out of his saddle.'

'You sure?'

'Shot him dead centre.'

Dallas Zimmer rubbed his big veined hands together. He applauded, 'A good night's work, Heck.' He warned however, 'But just remember to keep your trap shut about everything.'

Halliday said smugly, 'You can rely on me, Mr Zimmer.'

'I'll make sure you get double paydirt this month, Heck,' Zimmer said, promising to reward his man. 'Now stable your horse, scrub up and join the party. See that Mex gal on the veranda?'

Halliday's eyes widened. 'The one filling wine glasses?'

'Señorita Maria,' Zimmer supplied her name.

The Mexican girl was slim, raven-haired, hardly out of her teens.

'A mighty fine looking gal, even if she is a Mex,' Halliday remarked, his dark eyes raking her.

'She's yours for the night,' Zimmer said, grinning. 'You'll enjoy what she has to offer – and I should know.' Maria had warmed his bed since Penelope died but he wouldn't need her anymore. His wedding to Sierra was so close now he could wait. 'Just tell her I said she had to look after you.'

'Thanks, Mr Zimmer.'

Gleefully, Halliday led his horse towards the stable.

'You're mighty generous tonight, Boss,' O'Neill remarked.

'Heck did us all a good turn,' the rancher said. 'Actually showed some guts for once.'

'Damn shame about Scurlock and the boys.'

The rancher shrugged. 'Not really, Pat. We've had that outlaw bunch on our payroll for a while now. Too long, in fact. Been considering for a while how we can cut our ties with them. Seems Dawson obliged us.'

O'Neill chuckled, 'And then Heck got rid of Dawson.'

'He sure did,' Zimmer chuckled.

'That all, boss?'

'Go back and celebrate, Pat.'

Dallas Zimmer downed the last drops of wine remaining in his glass.

It was indeed a time to celebrate. He congratulated himself. He was not only about to marry the best-looking woman in Spanish Wells but any hindrances to his ambition to expand his cattle empire had all been removed.

Lance Corporal Honani could have started poking around and causing trouble after seeing Triple Z cattle grazing on what he believed was Navajo land. Folks might even have been supportive of a Union soldier hero. But now he was out of the way . . . forever. Furthermore, the Scurlock outlaw gang had long outlived their usefulness to him, and he'd always been concerned that one day some meddling lawmen would hunt them down, and that one of them, Thompson probably, might blab.

While George wore the badge in Spanish Wells, that wouldn't happen, but his lazy son might not always want to be town sheriff.

But what if someday that psalm-singing deputy took over? Unlike many men, Kel Blake wouldn't be bought, that was for sure.

As for Luke Dawson, he'd loomed as the biggest trouble of them all.

He was the kind of man who'd poke around. If he'd found out about what had happened to his family and friends on Wild Wolf Ridge and if he'd probed even deeper about Sundown Valley, he would have presented a big threat. Yes, he owed Halliday for the well-aimed bullet that had left Dawson for buzzard-bait. He might even let him have Maria on a permanent basis.

As Elijah announced he was about to sing 'Wrestlin' Jacob', Dallas Zimmer let his thoughts drift to Dawson's Bar LD land. He'd been there more than once. Good grazing land, although his fence needed fixing. Maybe he could run some of his cattle there. Who would be there to stop him? No one. Might be a prelude to taking over all of Wild Wolf Ridge.

Things were really falling into place for him. He was

marrying Dawson's woman and he'd make plans to grab Dawson's prime land. Tonight was a real celebration!

The smirking rancher sauntered back to his guests as Elijah began to sing about Jacob. He saw Sierra smiling, waiting for him. It had been a great night for her. Everyone had been congratulating his future bride.

Moistening his dry, cracked lips, Zimmer told himself she would soon be standing beside him on their wedding day, then in his bed. Everything was working out just fine.

CHAPTER EIGHT

Night was in retreat as the first pink light of dawn flushed the eastern rim of the valley, and with the new day Luke Dawson slowly regained consciousness. At first all he knew was pain throbbing like a heavy drum in his back and then it all came back to him: the sudden shock of that bullet ripping into his back, the quick glimpse of Heck Halliday and finally his own descent into darkness. He gritted his teeth and slowly opened his eyes.

That's when he heard grunts and hissing and felt a tentative scraping on his lower back, right below where the bullet had lodged. Dark, ominous shadows flitted across his blurred vision.

There was another sharp scrape, then a jab right into his open wound. He saw two ugly claws right in front of his eyes and he lashed out with his fist, striking the hungry buzzard's mantle and knocking the scavenger off its feet. The other buzzard pecking at his raw, bloody wound immediately flew into the air and hovered overhead, protesting and grunting at being denied its meal.

As more daylight came in a flood, Luke saw the gun that he'd dropped. It had bounced under sagebrush.

100

Racked with stabbing pain, Luke dragged himself to the bush and grabbed his Peacemaker. It felt cold yet so welcome in his hand, but the buzzards were already abandoning him in favour of the three other bodies littering this shallow outlaw valley, so he didn't need to fire a shot.

He felt dizzy, head spinning like a crazy wagon wheel. Then he heard the whinny of a horse.

Red Jack was right where he'd been left, the other side of the big boulder. Luke called out the chestnut's name and Wishbone's well-trained horse trotted to him.

Luke tried to stand but at first the effort was too much. His knees crumbled, blood dripped from his wounded back, then he fell headlong to the earth. He knew he had to get out of here and the only way was on Red Jack's back. He raised himself to his knees, steadying himself by clinging to the left side stirrup strap. Red Jack whinnied as Luke reached up to find the saddle. Clutching leather, Luke slowly hauled himself up to stand beside the big chestnut.

'Steady, boy,' Luke spoke softly and reassuringly to the horse.

Red Jack stayed right where he was, enabling Luke to find the saddle horn. Still talking in low tones to the chestnut, Luke managed to lift his left boot into the stirrup. Sweat beaded his brow and his wound was a cesspool of agony, but Luke summoned every ounce of strength and levered himself up into the saddle where he sat fighting the waves of pain flowing like a surging flood through his body.

Finally, he ordered the chestnut. 'Home, Red Jack, home.'

Leaning forward, Luke Dawson started riding at walking pace back across the valley. Leaving three bodies to the buzzards, he retraced his trail to the valley rim and then followed his tracks to the banks of the slow-moving river. Pain gnawed at his back. At times the dizziness almost claimed him and darkness overhung him like a cloud, but he was determined not to die out here in the wilderness. There were important things he had to do.

First, Honani's Medal of Honour needed to find its rightful home and Luke had already resolved to take it to the Navajo's family, hopefully in Na Dené Canyon. Many men would ask why he'd bother to do this. But they hadn't served alongside one of the bravest, most loyal soldiers to fight for the Union. If they had, they wouldn't even think of asking that question.

However, there were questions Luke wanted answers to. Was Honani murdered just for his medal? He thought that was unlikely. And if robbery was the only motive, why had Heck Halliday ridden with this bunch of outlaws? Halliday was on the Triple Z payroll. Surely he earned enough punching Zimmer's beeves? Or maybe Zimmer was somehow bound up with them? That was more likely, Luke considered grimly. Zimmer probably used these outlaws to do his dirtiest work.

He began to ford the river. It ran slowly but was deep and the water crept higher than his boots in their stirrups. The river's coldness was in direct contrast to the fire in his back, a fire that was spreading down his spine and seeping through into his chest. Blood was still flowing, smudging the saddle and dripping into the river.

He felt tired, a dangerous kind of weariness because he had to stay in the saddle. Reeds brushed Luke's body as Red Jack reached the western bank.

Noon saw him cross the rye grass flats. By mid-after-

102

noon, he rode into the shadows of the twin mountain peaks, heading for the creek that threaded through Whispering Pass. The bullet in his back felt like a heavy stone and his shirt was now soaked with blood. He knew he couldn't dismount, even to give Red Jack a rest, because he no longer had the strength to get back into the saddle. So he just kept riding, even slower now. Trees, rocks, ferns, running water all merged together.

After crossing the creek, he felt as if his life was ebbing away. Dusk settled over the high country. He saw hungry white eyes in the darkness, then the howling of wolf packs. They could smell the blood and he knew they were closing in. He simply had to cling to Red Jack's head as the horse stumbled. Luke was no longer sure of the trail and his eyes were so blurred he'd have trouble seeing it anyway, so he just let the big chestnut drift through the forest.

Two hours fled.

He gripped his Peacemaker in case the savage wolves were bold enough to close around old Red Jack.

It was almost midnight when clouds cloaked the moon. One by one the stars disappeared, but when the night was darkest he caught the glimpse of a distant light. Suddenly a pine branch lashed him, lifting him clean from his saddle and dumping him over the tree's protruding roots.

Luke just managed to pull the trigger of his Peacemaker and fire a single shot into the sky.

Then he blacked out.

When Luke Dawson finally opened his eyes he saw Annie's face.

She was perched on the side of his bunk and smiling down at him.

103

'I knew you'd make it, Luke Dawson,' she said happily. Her deep blue eyes sparkled like diamonds. 'Pa figured you would, too.' She winked at him. 'He said you were a tough old . . . Well, Pa said I needed to learn to be a lady so I won't say the cuss word he used.'

For a long moment Luke just stared at her, hardly believing he was alive and looking at Wishbone's daughter.

'How long . . . have I been . . . here?' Luke asked in a husky voice.

'Two nights ago Pa heard a gunshot,' Annie told him. 'It was real close by Widow Rose's place.' Luke recalled the light he'd seen just before he'd ridden into that tree. Annie explained, 'When Pa and the widow went looking, they saw Red Jack and then you on the ground. They brought you back here and . . . and then Pa told me to sharpen a knife.'

'So Wishbone cut my bullet out?'

She shook her head. 'Nope, I did.'

'You did?'

'Pa and the widow had too much whiskey in their bellies to have steady hands so they gave me the chore,' Annie said, smiling. 'Wasn't real difficult. They turned you over for me, I said my first prayer for years and slipped the knifepoint in. Wasn't easy because the blood gushed. Managed to find the bullet and flick it out. If you want the bullet for a keepsake, it's in Pa's ashtray.'

'Then I owe you my life, Annie,' Luke said gratefully.

Using his elbows, Luke started to lever himself up so he could sit with his back propped against a pillow. He took his time because every fibre of his body protested.

'Careful, Luke! You're not fit and well yet!' she warned.

All the same, he managed to sit up. Pain drummed from

104

his back but it was nowhere near as sharp and strong as when he'd ridden back here. It was steady but muted, the pain a man feels when he's on the mend. And yet, Luke knew he was weakened, drained of energy and he ought to have rest. It was then, quite suddenly, he realized he was naked under the blanket that covered him.

It was as if she read his thoughts.

Her cheeks reddening, she said, 'I washed the spare clothes you had in your saddle pack. I'll fetch them for you. Uh, Luke, you might need some help to put them on. Pa only went out to check his traps so he won't be long.'

'I can get dressed myself.'

'I doubt it, Luke,' she argued, hands on hips.

'My clothes, Annie,' he reminded her.

She swept out of the room, quickly returning with his neatly folded, faded blue shirt and Levis. He noted approvingly that new wooden buttons had been sewn on the shirt where previously two were missing. And a certain tear in the left leg of his pants had been stitched up. He glanced at her again. In that moment he caught her eyes looking wistfully at his bare chest that showed above the blanket.

'I guess you can manage,' Annie relented, a hint of disappointment in her voice. 'I'll brew some coffee while you put your clothes on.' She paused at the door and said sternly, 'But stay right here, on your bed.'

'Sure, Doc Annie,' he said, grinning.

'And you're still my patient,' she reminded him.

Annie was a fine young woman, he told himself once again as she went to the parlour. She'd certainly done a fine job of patching him up. He felt behind his back. The wound was still swollen but he knew it was already healing. It took him a full minute but he managed to ignore the jabs of pain and put on his shirt, followed by the pants. He stood up and took three paces to the window.

'Luke!' she scolded him from the doorway. Then she laughed. 'If I was your woman I'd—' Suddenly embarrassed at uttering those hasty words, she stopped short and said softly, 'Sorry for that! Don't take any notice of what I said, Luke Dawson. Please join me in the parlour.'

He walked unaided to the table by her wood stove.

They talked over coffee and her home-baked cookies until Wishbone barged his way inside with two dead squirrels slung over his left shoulder.

'The saints be praised! You made it!' Wishbone welcomed him.

'Thanks to both of you,' Luke said gratefully.

'Tell me all about what happened, Luke,' Wishbone insisted, straddling the chair on the opposite side of the table. 'And before you ask, your friend Honani is under the clay on your land, close to your brother and his wife. Widow Rose read some words from her mother's prayer book and I dug the grave. Not sure if the Navajo was a believer, but I planted a cross anyway.'

Luke told them both what had happened to him: how he'd tracked the killers to the outlaw canyon and shot them. Wishbone raised his craggy eyebrows when he mentioned Heck Halliday being there. Drinking his coffee, Luke then recalled the bullet in his back and his desperate ride back.

'When Pa found you, the medal was hanging from your shirt pocket,' Annie said when he'd finished. 'It's here, safe, in Pa's room with your guns.'

'Which you won't be needing for a while,' Wishbone said.

'Pa's right,' Annie backed him. 'Rest is what you need.'

'A week, maybe more,' her father said firmly.

'I'm obliged to you both,' Luke said, drinking her coffee, 'but I can't stay for a week. I have a chore that can't wait.'

'Such as?' Wishbone asked.

'First, I intend to take that medal to Na Dené Canyon.'

'That's two days' ride, probably three or four in your condition,' Wishbone protested. 'And the trail goes plumb through Apache territory.'

'While I was away at the war, the Navajos left their land in Sundown Valley. No one seems to know where they went, but before we parted, Honani said their tribe originally hailed from Na Dené. He figured that's the only place they could be. That Medal of Honour belongs with them.'

Wishbone shook his head disapprovingly. 'I've heard the Apaches have a new renegade chief. They call him Blood Knife; dresses like a Mexican but he's Apache through and through. By all accounts, he's a real scalp-hunter when it comes to raiding white folks.'

'Reckon we had a passing acquaintance with him on the trail to Spanish Wells.' Luke recalled the running gunfight with an Apache in Mexican garb and his riders.

'He's slippery as a snake,' Wishbone warned. 'Don't tangle with him.'

'Please, Luke, Pa's right,' Annie pleaded fervently.

Luke rested for that whole day, feeling his strength returning with every hour. Later that afternoon he took a short walk outside in the forest. Annie joined him as he checked his bay horse in the stable and then cleaned his rifle. When she saw him with his gun she knew further talk was useless. He'd made up his mind.

When morning came Luke felt stiff, but the wound was healing and the pain had been reduced to a distant throb. He dressed, strapped on his gun belt and slid the Peacemaker into his holster. Annie rose early too, donning her dressing gown so she could light the stove and fry salted bacon for his breakfast while he saddled Buck. They shared a meal together. Then Luke slipped the Navajo's medal back into his shirt pocket and made ready to leave.

It was cloudy outside and the wind coming down from the mountains was cold enough to chill a man's bones. Annie handed him a bag packed with jerky, hardtack, fried beans and half a dozen sugar cookies she'd baked especially the previous night. Luke was about to mount up as Annie took a quick glance at the track to the widow's cabin. Her father was still up there but he'd be back any minute, so what she yearned all night to do had to be done very quickly.

She walked right up to Luke, stood on the tips of her toes and kissed him long and hard. And he kissed her back. Trembling at her own boldness but meaning every passionate moment of that kiss, she stepped away so he could mount his bay horse.

She blurted, 'Come back to me, Luke Dawson! Please come back!'

Luke picked up his reins and rode north for the distant mountains.

CHAPTER NINE

Luke Dawson rode through Whispering Pass, slowing, then lingering for a long moment at the scene of Honani's brutal slaying. The moaning wind had already blown fallen leaves over the charred remains of his campfire. It was justice that most of the Navajo's sneaky murderers were now dead. He had no time for back-shooters. To blast a man in the back was a low, cowardly act and Scurlock's outlaws only got what was coming to them. As for Halliday, he'd keep.

He nudged Buck and rode higher into the lonely pass. Here the twin peaks looked down on him as he followed the creek to its source, a rock-rimmed lake being ruffled by the rising wind. Rounding the dark, deep water, Luke headed down out of the pass towards canyon country. The motion of riding a horse made his wound stretch and he could smell the small trickle of blood that oozed under Annie's bandage. But he kept riding, right through to dusk when he found a sheltered hollow inside a copse of towering cottonwoods.

Heeding Wishbone's warning about this being danger-ous Apache country, he decided not to light a fire, instead eating Annie's cooked meat cold and drinking water instead of coffee. He'd been used to such fare during the war so it brought back memories he hoped to forget one day when he settled down. And he certainly wanted to start life over again.

In the past, when he considered the future, Sierra naturally came into his mind, but tonight, sitting here with his back to a rough-barked pine tree, she wasn't in his thoughts. Instead, a rare smile cracked his lips as he remembered Annie's kiss. It might have been impulsive but she certainly meant it.

The night wore on, a midnight moon glimmered and a wolf pack howled behind him. Luke didn't sleep. He merely rested and watched the darkness.

First light saw him eat more of Annie's food and saddle Buck. He was hardly out of the canyon when he saw smoke. Drawing his bay horse under a rock ledge, he watched small puffs of grey smoke drift into the new light of day. They were coming from a timbered ridge south of the canyon trail he was taking. Even as he watched, more smoke rose, this second signal coming from a rim that protruded over the trail itself.

Waiting under this ledge, Luke raised his eyes to the distant west where the ancient, majestic red butte Honani often spoke of stood tall and lonely, presiding over Na Dené canyon. If he kept on this trail that led straight towards the butte, it would take him about two days to ride there. To circle north and keep well clear of the Indians sending these smoke signals, he'd add an extra day, maybe longer, to his journey. Even then, there was still a risk he'd be spotted by Apache hunters. Of course, he might have been seen already. He decided to stay on the trail he was following.

Keeping to the shadows of the canyon wall, he rode slowly and quietly towards the rim where the nearest smoke signal was rising. When he was much closer, he drew Buck into a cleft in the grey granite rock.

Smelling the smoke, he waited.

Lifting his Peacemaker from its leather, he eased himself from the saddle, edged out of the cleft and saw the Indian on the rim. The Apache was an older man, lean as a rake, wearing a cavalry tunic and pants he'd doubtless taken from a dead trooper.

Luke knew he couldn't just stay holed up here. He had to make his move, so he climbed a narrow track that steeped up to the rim. Once he levered his body onto the crest, he was able to look over the canyon country stretching west and see the much loftier timbered ridge where the other smoke was rising from. Luke figured that this other Apache, now concealed in the timber, had spotted the lone white man riding and sent a smoke signal to the wrinkled warrior who was just a few feet from him now.

The Apache warrior cast a shadow over his small fire. He was watching the trail below like a bird of prey, watching and waiting, anticipating that the unsuspecting white man would ride beneath him. He might be old but he could still fire his rifle and kill.

Luke lifted his gun from its leather. He didn't want to shoot the Indian. Apart from his reluctance to kill any man of his advancing years, the thunder of his gun could most likely bring other hostile Apaches to this canyon. Accordingly, Luke kept his head low and walked slowly and noiselessly towards the old Indian crouched next to his small fire.

He was less than half a dozen paces away when the

111

Apache turned his head. Instinctively, the Indian reached for his knife but a split moment later Luke was on him. The Apache grabbed his knife but before he could use it, Luke's Peacemaker flashed in the early sunlight and cracked into the side of his head. The Indian stumbled, dropped to the flat rock, out like a snuffed light.

Luke took the knife from the Indian's clenched fist, stamped out the fire until only wisps of smoke remained, then dragged the unconscious man back from the rim's edge. Leaving the would-be ambusher on the ground, Luke climbed down and mounted his waiting horse.

Riding under the rim, he passed the place where he could well have been gunned down, then pushed west towards the red butte. Emerging from a shallow canyon, he started across a high mesa.

High noon saw him well clear of the timbered ridge where smoke signals had ceased to rise two hours ago, but just when he'd stopped to rest Buck, he saw the rising cloud of dust in his wake. He was being followed, most likely by that other Apache warrior who'd been sending up smoke signals.

Luke kept riding the mesa, a sloping tableland cluttered with cottonwoods. He found a clump of trees and halted Buck in their shade. Disturbed, two angry fat sidewinders slid slowly away into a rocky crevice. He heard their rattle, then silence as he flattened himself to a cottonwood and waited.

Within minutes the Apache came into sight. This one, although stumpy, was much younger than the warrior he'd knocked unconscious earlier this morning. His sharp eyes were reading Buck's clear tracks as he headed across the mesa. Luke had hoped to slip into Navajo country without a hostile encounter, but this earnest warrior had latched onto his tracks and was unlikely to give up this opportunity to kill a paleface intruder and bring himself accolades and honour.

Luke watched as the rider came closer. He was bronze-skinned, longhaired, and naked to the waist. There was a chain of white animal bones around his muscular neck and he clutched a long rifle that gleamed in the hot sun.

The Apache brave halted his pony twenty paces away, looked directly at the cottonwoods and levelled his gun. Luke stepped into the open. Two rifles fired in unison, breaking the mesa silence. Luke's bullet bored into the Apache's ribs, blasting him clean out of his cloth saddle. Simultaneously, the warrior's slug splintered into the cottonwood, less than an inch from the white man's face. Clutching his wound, the Apache charged him on foot.

Luke held his ground, levelled his rifle a second time and pulled the trigger, this time shooting him high in the chest. The Indian pitched sideways, sprawled over a clump of bluegrass.

With the gunshot echoes fading over the mesa, Luke dragged the body into the cottonwoods. The Apache's pony had already run off.

Luke remounted Buck and rode out of the cottonwoods. He was sure the gunfire would have been heard by other Apaches, but he reached the far side of the mesa without seeing more raised dust.

There, with dusk falling, he made night camp in an arroyo. Again, he lit no fire. He listened to the nocturnal sounds of the wilderness – the bark-like grunts of squirrels, the rustle of lizards in grass, the eerie hooting of a couple of horned owls high in their cottonwood trees. Luke had heard stories that Apaches never fought at night but he was taking no chances. He would keep awake all night, which wasn't difficult. He'd learned to live without sleep during the war.

Luke was back in the saddle when first light showed. He rode down from the mesa and gave an Apache village a wide berth. The red butte towering over canyon country loomed larger, much closer, as he followed a dry wash. He was riding easier now, with only the occasional prick of pain coming from his back.

Twice he saw Apache riders. He'd been expecting them. By now the old Indian nursing a sore head would be back at his village and barking coyotes would have lured angry warriors to the body in the cottonwood trees. They would be looking for him sure enough.

And so Luke sheltered in a jumble of rocks as three rode by and later, mid-afternoon, he glanced at his back-trail and glimpsed over a dozen others combing the western rim of the mesa he'd crossed. They were closing in on him.

It was almost sundown and the red butte he was headed for was wreathed in crimson shadow. There were other shadows too, shadows that moved along the crest of a lonely ridge within rifle range of where he was riding. He reached the gaping mouth of a narrow pass that spilled over a slope leading right down to the big butte. Riding swiftly in the dusk through the passage, he heard the hooting of owls, human owls calling to each other. One was real close, from a cave in the wall of the pass. Next moment a bullet sang past Buck's head and ricocheted off a boulder. Another winged wide, a third whined overhead.

Luke urged his bay horse into a lope, racing down the

long slope. The gunfire died on the wind but as Luke
headed for the butte, he turned in the saddle and saw a
line of mounted Apaches. One of them was the renegade
chief, Blood Knife, whose Mexican clothes he could see
plainly in the last light of day. The Apache leader brandished his rifle in a show of furious defiance and Luke
knew that any journey back through Blood Knife's country
would now be very dangerous indeed.

For now, though, Luke simply put distance between
Apache territory and himself, steering Buck around the
base of the big butte. Below him stretched the Navajo
canyons. Even from here he could see the glow of lamps
and fires.

Less than one hour later Luke reached a long adobe
brick building with a string of lanterns across its front. The
sign announcing MORMON MISSION GENERAL STORE
painted in dark blue hung over the open door, reminding
Luke that Honani once told him church missionaries had
come to these canyons with high hopes of converting the
Navajo tribes to their religion.

Luke slowed his bay gelding. Burros and a single horse
stood patiently along the tie rail while a mangy dog barked
incessantly, warning those inside that a visitor had just
ridden in out of the night.

He emptied his saddle as a bald, pot-bellied man in a
check shirt and wide pants loomed large as Goliath in the
doorway. The storekeeper scrutinised Luke through his
dark-rimmed glasses and decided it was unlikely the
stranger was of their faith. However, the Mormon seemed
friendly enough.

'Welcome to our mission, gentile friend. You've come a
long way?'

'From Sundown Valley,' Luke told him, securing Buck to the rail.

'Ah, one of my sweet wives came from the town of Spanish Wells, near that valley,' the Mormon said amicably.

Luke didn't need to be reminded that many of Brigham Young's Mormon pioneers who'd come west to Utah were indeed polygamists. He didn't hold with having more than one woman himself but he wasn't here for a religious argument.

He decided to come straight to the point. 'I'm looking for Navajos who probably arrived here and settled in Na Dené Canyon a couple of years ago. They belong to the Armijo clan.'

'Yes, I know them,' the storekeeper said immediately. 'Chief Nastas and his people. Fine folk!'

Luke felt both elated and relieved when he heard the name of Honani's father. The Armijo clan might have been driven from their village in Sundown Valley but at least they were here, in their ancestral canyon. He was at trail's end. Now he could let the family know the grim news of Honani's terrible death and in addition he would also be able to deliver the Medal of Honour. It was the least he could do for a fellow soldier.

'I would like to see them,' Luke announced.

'You are a friend of Chief Nastas?' the Mormon asked.

'Yes, I rode with his son, Honani,' Luke informed him.

'The Armijo rarely come into our general store,' the Mormon said, adding regretfully, 'and none come to church.' He paused before saying, 'Chief Nastas is ageing but he's still alive and well. Sadly, not many of his family arrived here with him – I'd say ten, maybe a dozen, that's all. I seem to remember one squaw had twin boys several

116

months ago.'

Hearing this, Luke merely stared at him. When he'd ridden through Sundown Valley on the day he'd left to fight in the civil war, there had been at least eighty men, women and children living in their Navajo village. Had smallpox struck them? He'd heard of entire frontier communities wiped out by the disease.

'I'll ride to Na Dené,' Luke decided.

'Come inside first,' the storekeeper invited amicably. 'We offer hospitality to all. We Mormons do not hold with coffee drinking, as you may know, but we keep Arbuckle for gentile riders passing through. You can have a drink on the house while I explain where Na Dené Canyon is.'

'Thank you, friend,' Luke accepted his offer.

The smiling Mormon did more than offer him a drink.

While the youngest of his three wives, a buxom young girl in her mid teens, brought him a cup of Arbuckle on a tray, the Mormon storekeeper, who introduced himself as Elder Micah James, used pen and ink to sketch directions on parchment paper. The mission church, he explained, was just down the road from this general store, although he admitted not many Navajos had been converted, preferring their tribal beliefs. To get to Na Dené Canyon, Luke had to take the southern fork behind the church and negotiate a labyrinth of canyons to reach Na Dené. There he'd find a camp with just two hogans. This was where the last remnants of the Armijo clan lived.

'It's a long trail to Na Dené,' Elder James told him as his second wife, heavily pregnant, brought Luke chilli bean stew, which she assured him was also 'on the house'. Micah James added, 'Would it not be better to stop here for the night? We have rooms for travellers. Two dollars a night includes bath, breakfast and a copy of the Book of Mormon by our founder, Joseph Smith, included.'

The elder's first wife, an elderly grey-haired woman dressed in sombre black, who stood like a holy stature behind the store counter, held up their sacred book for him to see. Luke was tempted, not by the book, but by the notion of a bed. He'd come a long way without any rest and he could see these Mormon missionaries really wanted to chat. In this remote, far-away mission, they rarely met up with white folks. However, Luke decided he wasn't going to rest until he came face-to-face with Chief Nastas and his family, even if it was after midnight.

'Appreciate the offer, but I need to ride.'

All the same, he insisted on paying for his soup and drink.

With the Mormon's map in his pocket, Luke rode away from the general store, passed the small stone chapel and schoolhouse and headed into the night. He threaded through some empty stockyards and rode by the first Navajo village where he counted over thirty brush lodges dotted around a large cooking fire. The aroma of roasting venison wafted to him on the rising wind. Following the Mormon's map, Luke probed deeper into canyon country. Many of the walled-in valleys were small and easy to cross in mere minutes; some were wider, home to more than one Navajo village. The rising moon cast ghostly shadows over the trail as he followed the northern wall of a twisting canyon with a floor of gritty sand. Still he rode while the cold wind moaned like a dying man.

Finally, one hour to midnight, the trail narrowed through a steep-walled pass and followed a twisting slope down to a sheltered canyon.

The map showed him this was Na Dené.

Luke saw a solitary fire in this canyon. It wasn't blazing like some of the others he'd seen, but burning low, only just glimmering bravely in the night.

He rode across the valley towards the small fire where two brush hogans were huddled close together in its glow. He passed half a dozen goats by a water trough in their fenced corral. Looking past the corral, he saw four figures hunched over the dying fire. He heard no talk and he saw no movement. One of the Navajos, an old man sitting cross-legged, smoked a long pipe.

Luke knew him. He was Honani's father, Nastas, grey-haired, wrinkled, his hooded eyes shut tight as though he was asleep. Right alongside him was another elderly Navajo whom Luke recognized as the one-eyed medicine man he'd once known in Sundown Valley. He didn't know the other two but they were both old. Three squaws sat together out front of the smallest lodge, watching children play quietly in the dust. Another woman stood alone drinking from an earthen cup. He could smell redeye whiskey, the scourge of many Indian communities. The woman looked up from her cup as Luke rode in, but she hardly gave him a second glance.

Luke told himself there was little real life in this community. It was as if a sombre cloud had descended on the men and women who'd once been living happily in Sundown Valley.

The medicine man saw Luke's approach. He poked Nastas who responded by opening his eyes wide as the white man from the past rode unheralded into their fire-lit circle. Even as Luke halted his bay horse, Honani's youngest brother, Shiye, came running like a deer from the

119

large hogan. At least he had some life! He was now twenty years old, a muscular, bare-chested young man wearing a blue tunic and patched cotton pants bought from the Mormon Store.

'Luke Dawson!' Shiye welcomed him in a booming voice that echoed over the canyon. He stood there impatiently as Luke dismounted. He kept looking into the darkness Luke had just emerged from, expecting another rider to loom out of the night. He demanded, 'My brother, Honani?'

Chief Nastas was helped to his feet by two of the other men while Honani's mother emerged limping from her domed hogan.

Luke waited for Nastas and his wife to join them.

'Honani is dead,' Luke told them.

Honani's mother let out a high-pitched wail, then buried her head in her hands while Nastas and his surviving son, Shiye, stood in the flickering firelight. The chief's face was impassive, drained of blood. Shocked at the terrible news, Chief Nastas swayed on his feet, in danger of toppling over, but Shiye managed to hold his father steady.

'My son . . . killed in . . . in white man's war!' Nastas said hoarsely, shaking his head in disbelief.

'He wasn't killed in the war,' Luke said quietly.

'What do you mean, Luke Dawson?'

'He survived the war, like I did,' Luke explained.

'Then what happened?' Shiye demanded.

Luke told them, 'Honani was murdered, shot in the back soon after he came home from the war.'

Honani's mother wept bitter tears as the other women gathered around, attempting to console her.

Chief Nastas, visibly shaking, addressed Luke hoarsely above his squaw's cries. 'Come, sit with us at the council fire.'

It was an honour to be asked to join the elders and Luke left the bay gelding for the women to tether. Out of respect for the Navajo chief, he waited for Nastas to resume his place before sitting opposite him. At his father's bidding, Shiye joined them. Knowing Navajo custom, Luke maintained his silence, waiting until the chief spoke first.

'Tell me what happened,' Nastas said, his tone laced with grief.

'We rode first to Spanish Wells, then to Sundown Valley where we expected to see your village,' Luke recalled their homecoming. 'Honani was distressed when he saw that his people had gone.' The Navajo elders were silent, staring disconsolately into the dying fire as he told them about the confrontation with the Triple Z men just over the creek. 'Rancher Zimmer said he'd taken over your land because you'd just abandoned your village and vanished. That's when we parted. I rode to Wild Wolf Ridge, and Honani decided to come here, to Na Dené, to see what he could find out. Later in the night I heard shooting. Together with Wishbone – you'll remember the old trapper sure enough – we found Honani dead with bullets in his back. The filthy back-shooters had murdered him. They had their reasons for killing him and they also stole this. . . .' Luke lifted Honani's medal from his pocket. 'General Ulysses S. Grant presented this Medal of Honour to your son, Honani, for extreme bravery.' He handed the medal to the Navajo chief who clutched it to his chest.

After Chief Nastas thanked him, Luke recalled how subsequently he'd retrieved the stolen medal and then tracked across Apache country to find the Armijo people.

'We are all who are left,' Shiye told him.

'The last of the Armijo tribe,' Nastas lamented.

'So what in the hell happened?' Luke asked them bluntly.

Nastas called for drinks and food to be brought for the elders and their visitor. Luke knew better than to press him for immediate answers, so he waited. One old squaw left comforting Honani's mother and brought them corn cakes and white man's Arbuckle mixed with goats' milk.

'Our enemies, Blood Knife's Apaches, came out of mountains, attacked us,' Nastas told him. 'We killed three of their raiding party but as they rode away, they snatched two of our women. One was Johona, my wife of many years. You see her weeping now. She often weeps.' He added, 'I rode after the kidnappers with my son Shiye and six braves.'

Shiye took up the story from his father. 'For two moons we hunted our Apache enemies deep inside their territory. Finally, there was a battle. We killed ten of the enemy before Blood Knife and the rest of his spineless snakes escaped. Four of our Navajo warriors lost their lives but we rescued our squaws. As we were returning, we heard much shooting, the sound of many, many bullets being fired in Sundown Valley. But we were a long way from our lodges. We hastened but we were too late. When we arrived back in valley, our homes were burning, our people were gone – all of them, warriors, squaws, children. That is, all except Medicine Man Kachina, who saw it all.'

Kachina lowered his eyes, saying nothing, remembering.

'I was there when white men came by night, attacked our village.' The medicine man spoke mournfully, looking deeply into the dying embers of their fire. 'Most of us were asleep. Paleface Zimmer was there with many riders.' He held up two hands, fingers extended, signifying the number ten. 'They had big gun in wagon. Very, very big. I had not seen this gun before. It took four men to work this gun. It shot many bullets, *bang, bang, bang, bang, bang*, very quick!'

'Goddamn Gatling gun,' Luke figured. 'Started to use them in the war. They fire five bullets a second.'

'Many Navajo braves die, slaughtered in their beds. I had been sleeping with the spirits of our forefathers in sacred cave. A white man, the one called O'Neill, came into the cave with his rifle. He shot me in the neck. Look!' Kachina ran his finger along the length of a deep puffy scar that made a slash under his jaw. He excused himself. 'I could do nothing. I was wounded, I had no weapon. I pretended to be dead.'

Luke glimpsed the hint of a sneer crease Shiye's face. Along with his father and others, Shiye had always reckoned that Kachina laid low to save his own neck, but despite their contempt for him, the coward was the tribe's medicine man with healing powers, so nothing had been said out loud. Kachina, however, had been fully believed when he described the brutal, bloody massacre of virtually the whole village: men, women and children. There was no reason for him to lie about that, and besides, three squaws who'd hidden in the creek reeds backed him up. They were here tonight in Na Dené Canyon.

'After big gun stopped firing, Zimmer's riders went from lodge to lodge, shooting everyone in them, even the very old,' Kachina recalled.

Luke Dawson felt sick in the pit of his belly, sick and angry, as he imagined screaming children and terrified women being ruthlessly gunned down. He was sure the

Navajo warriors would have fought bravely but they'd faced overwhelming odds. Not only had Zimmer's men attacked while they were mostly asleep but they'd procured a deadly Gatling gun to pump hot lead into the helpless village. What took place had been the indiscriminate massacre of virtually a whole tribe. All because of Dallas Zimmer's greedy lust for more land.

'When killing was over, the white eyes carried bodies to wagon, took them away,' the medicine man said. 'Then they set fire to our homes.'

There was silence around the Navajo fire as Luke struggled with the very notion of white settlers murdering a whole clan of Indians and then burning their village to the ground. He could imagine sidewinders like Zimmer doing this, but what about the other men? Maybe they'd just gone along with it all. He'd seen what war could do to normally decent men, but no soldier he'd fought alongside, or even against, would stoop to slaughtering women and children in their beds. It must have been a night of terrible evil. Surely some of those killers at least would be living with dark guilt? Or maybe not. Zimmer had hired ruthless outlaws like the Scurlock bunch to shoot war hero Honani in the back, so maybe he'd mostly paid scum like them for the massacre.

'Did anyone else witness what happened?' Luke asked.

Chief Nastas and his son exchanged glances.

'Many white men who lived on Wild Wolf Ridge, where your land is, must have heard and seen what happened,' Shiye stated.

'And now most of them are dead,' Luke told them.

He thought of Caleb and Susan, his family. Then there were Lew Harbinger and the McPhersons, all decent folks.

They'd all lived on Wild Wolf Ridge, overlooking the Sundown Valley – now all dead. Maybe, Luke thought grimly, they'd all heard and seen too much and were killed before they talked.

'You said there were three squaws hidden by the creek.'

Shiye nodded at the women who were looking after the children.

'They saw everything that happened.'

Luke glanced at them. Two were frail and elderly, the third had a swollen belly, reminding him of Susan, his sister-in-law. When Heck Halliday shot Susan, he killed two people, her and her unborn infant. But Halliday's time would come, he promised himself – sooner rather than later.

He looked back down at the smoking embers of the Navajo cooking fire.

The only living witnesses to the brutal massacre in Sundown Valley were a medicine man and three squaws, all Navajo Indians. Even if they'd agree to testify, which was unlikely, who'd listen to any of them? Certainly not Sheriff George Zimmer. And even if by some miracle Dallas Zimmer and his filthy killers were actually charged with mass murder, what white judge or jury would convict them?

Luke knew what he had to do: ride back to Spanish Wells and be judge, jury and executioner.

CHAPTER TEN

It was sunup when Luke Dawson stood by the still-warm ashes of last night's fire. After midnight Chief Nastas had offered him a blanket and a place inside the largest lodge, but Luke had been content to remain outside. Here, under the stars in Na Dené Canyon, he'd snatched some sleep, just for a few hours.

He'd been awake since first light. Now he picked up his saddle ready for the journey home.

The Navajo chief, too, emerged from his domed home before the others stirred from their sleep. He was still wearing Honani's medal around his neck.

The chief pointed to the saddle. 'You are leaving us?'

'Riding out now,' Luke confirmed.

'You are welcome to stay in our humble camp for as long as you wish,' the chief reminded him.

'I know this but I need to return,' Luke reaffirmed. He saddled his bay horse while Chief Nastas watched. 'Honani, your son and my friend, was a brave warrior. He earned that medal, so wear it with pride, Nastas.'

'Thank you again for bringing it to us,' Nastas said gratefully. 'It means a lot to me and the Armijo people – what's left of us.'

'Your tribe can rise again,' Luke reassured him.

'Here! In this dry, dusty canyon!'

'No, not here,' Luke said quietly. 'I'm talking about back in Sundown Valley, where you lived and hunted from for many years.'

The Navajo chief shook his head in derision. 'This is impossible. This is crazy talk.'

'Maybe, but maybe not,' Luke said, climbing into the saddle. He picked up his reins ready to ride. 'Farewell, Chief, but I aim to be back after I do what needs to be done.'

'Which trail will you take?'

'Same one that brought me here.'

'It leads through Apache country.'

'I know.'

The Navajo chief said solemnly, 'You were fortunate to make it here with your scalp still in place. If you ride back through Apache territory, you may not be so fortunate. There is talk around Navajo fires. Many of us believe Blood Knife and his warriors are gathering for a murder raid. For a whole week, smoke signals have been rising, not just near where you rode, but all over Apache territory. The talk says Blood Knife wants to be more feared than Cochise, chief of the Chiricahua Apaches. To do this he must prove himself to be a great leader, so they say he plans a big raid to bring back many scalps.'

'Does the talk say where this raid will take place?'

'You ask where Blood Knife will murder first?' Chief Nastas considered. 'Some of our Navajo elders, in Na Dené and other canyon camps, believe the Mormon Store may be his first strike. There are three other Mormon missions

127

within two days' ride from the pass. These missions have just six, maybe seven men and their wives. Those missionaries try to help us but who will help them if Blood Knife comes to kill?'

'The soldiers at Fort Beaver need to be told.'

'Fort Beaver is one week's ride from here,' the Navajo leader said. 'If one of our men rode there today it would be two weeks before the bluecoat soldiers arrive, and that's if they come straight away.'

'I'd send that man now,' Luke advised.

'You speak wise words, Luke Dawson.' The chief considered for a few moments before deciding, 'I will send my son, Shiye.'

'Also, I'd call a meeting of all the other Navajo leaders in these canyons. If you stick together, Blood Knife will see a big bunch of your warriors and think twice about attacking your people.'

Nastas spat into the dust. 'It is true Blood Knife would not fight a battle, warrior against warrior, but he will still raid our villages and then run like a dirty coyote. He will strike when we do not expect him to come. He will kill those who are helpless to defend themselves. He will capture women and children. And he will rape women like he raped my wife when she was captured by his filthy snakes in Sundown Valley.' His voice broke. 'She still bears the scars and the shame of being forced to lie with him.'

'There is no shame,' Luke told him quietly. 'It was not her fault.'

'I have told her this,' the Indian said.

'Keep telling her,' Luke advised, climbing into his saddle. Taking his reins, he said finally, 'And keep believing you'll return to Sundown Valley.'

'May the Great Spirit ride with you,' Nastas wished fervently.

Luke rode away, leaving the Navajo chief standing alone by the dying fire. He didn't look back, retracing his tracks back out of Na Dené Canyon.

With the new sun flooding the canyons with light, he rode swiftly to the Mormon chapel and passed the front of the general store. The Mormon Mission looked so quiet and peaceful. Elder Micah James and his family were obviously still snug in their beds, curtains drawn across, snatching a last few minutes sleep before commencing the day's work.

But Nastas was right. The Mission was in the shadow of the pass, making it a perfect target for Blood Knife and his renegade Apaches to strike. The Navajos had plenty of horses in their canyon villages so he hoped Shiye would ride to Fort Beaver without delay.

Luke climbed the slope and headed Buck into the gaping jaws of the pass.

A long eagle circled high over the ancient rims. Two coyotes slunk away at his approach. He rode deeper into the pass, following a dry creek bed. As he rode, he thought about the injustice done to the Armijo people. This was a violent frontier. On one side, he'd heard tales of wagon trains being ambushed with their pioneer settlers scalped and left for the buzzards, but there was another side too that was not often talked about. Consumed by greed, a few white men – like Dallas Zimmer and his riders – had wiped out whole clans of natives. Mostly these massacres were ignored and went unpunished, the memory of them finally lost in the mists of time, but not this one. Luke Dawson was going to make sure of that. But first he had to make it back through possible hostile territory to Sundown Valley.

Luke emerged from the pass and reached the jumble of rocks he'd sheltered amongst on his way to Na Dené. This was where those three Apaches had drifted by while he kept low, hidden from their sight. This morning he saw no smoke, no raised dust, no riders. All was silent – maybe too silent, he told himself. He was about to leave the rocks behind when he heard a single hoot, like the hoot of an owl, only owls rarely hooted in broad daylight.

He drew his bay horse back into the rocks.

There he waited, one hand on his rifle.

Suddenly he heard the sharp whinny of a pony.

Glancing over his shoulder, he saw a lone rider come out of the pass but he didn't need to lift his rifle. In fact he lowered the gun, because the rider was Shiye, the Navajo chief's son. The young Indian was riding a shaggy-maned piebald that raised wispy dust in the sunlight. Emerging from the rocks, Luke waited. With his pony snorting, the Navajo brave came right alongside the white man in a swirl of dust.

'Luke Dawson! We must talk!'

'I thought you'd be on your way to Fort Beaver.'

'Pah! Pah! My father wanted me to ride to the fort to fetch soldiers but that's an old man's chore. I sent the medicine man.'

'So you disobeyed your father?'

Shiye stated, 'You will remember my father forbade me to ride to your war with my brother Honani.'

Luke said, 'He figured you were too young. He probably thought he'd lost one son to the Apaches, Honani might not come back, so he didn't want to lose you.' He added significantly, 'Specially as he figured it was a white man's war.'

'I was sixteen then,' the Navajo brave said. He thumped his naked chest with a firm fist. 'Now Shiye is a man, a warrior. I make my own decisions. This morning, when my father returned to his hogan for more rest, I gave orders to the medicine man. As we speak, Kachina rides to the fort.'

'So why are you here?' Luke demanded.

'You need me,' Shiye said simply.

Just then Luke heard another hooting sound.

This one rose high and echoed over the mesa he'd been planning to ride across.

'Apache,' the Navajo said.

'Figured so.'

'And there are ten, maybe twenty of them,' Shiye told him.

'How do you know? I can't see any.'

'When you left Na Dené, I rode to our canyon rim. From there you can see three long ridges in Apache Country north of the pass. The third ridge is the highest. On cloudy day it is covered but there were no clouds this morning. You would not have seen riders from slope you rode, but I saw them. Many riders, Luke Dawson. They would have seen you. They know you're here.'

'And they surely know you're here too,' Luke reminded him.

'Shiye is not afraid.'

'Don't look now,' Luke said softly, 'but there are three of the varmints coming out of the pass right behind us.'

'Others will be ahead on the high mesa,' the Navajo predicted.

'So we're trapped between them.'

'I know this country better than you, Luke Dawson,' Shiye said. 'This is Apache territory but I often ride up

131

here.' He added, 'I have my reasons.'

'So what's your suggestion?'

'There is a narrow way through these rocks. Follow me.'

Shiye raked his piebald with his heels, pushing the pony towards a gap between the massive boulders. It was a mere slit in the rocks, not easily seen. A man would have to know it was here. Looking at the mesa ahead, Luke saw a smoke signal floating slowly into the azure sky. The Navajo was right. The Apaches were up there sure enough. He glanced back at the pass, noting the three warriors drifting their way.

Keeping his head low, he nudged Buck into a slow walk and followed Shiye to the gap. The Navajo rider squeezed between two bald boulders, waited for Luke and pointed to a grassy ledge. A second smoke signal drifted up from along the mesa rim as Shiye led the way over the dry grass to the mouth of a dark cave.

The Navajo rode straight into the cave.

Luke urged Buck inside, following the Indian's piebald pony down a twisting passage. The sharp clatter of shod hoofs sounded through the cavern. Suddenly a shaft of light caught them both. This cave had two entrances and Luke looked ahead to where the passage widened, then made a rainbow arch before spilling out over a grey ledge.

The two riders emerged from darkness to dazzling sunlight. They were in a small canyon wedged beneath the southern slope of the big sagebrush mesa. The two smoke signals were still rising, but further away. Shiye pointed to a track that hugged the foot of the mesa slope. They rode together down the ledge and joined the crumbling trail.

Luke checked over his shoulder. He saw no Apaches by the cave; the puffs of smoke were becoming even more distant. Had they given the Apaches the slip? The track forked away from the mesa and twisted through some junipers. A northerly wind sprang up, stirring the red dust. Just before noon they let their horses drink from a water-hole. After taking a swallow from his canteen, Luke checked their back-trail and the towering mesa. Not even a wisp of smoke. No dust rising. Only a heated silence.

But then he saw the lone Apache on the next rim. He was an old buck, lean, wearing only a breechcloth. Astride his pinto pony, he sat motionless, like a marble statue, carved against the azure sky. Like a raptor ready to swoop, the Apache was looking down the barrel of his rifle at the riders by the waterhole.

Luke didn't need to alert Shiye because the Navajo had seen him too. They both lifted their rifles but the wily old Apache, his gun already levelled, fired first, sending a shot into the shimmering water. Then he began backing his pony into some timber.

Shiye's bullet bored into a juniper trunk, blowing splinters of wood into the Apache's chest while Luke's lead ripped flesh from his left arm. The Apache's scream of pain carried to them from the rim. Moments later, he vanished into the timber cover and fired five shots in rapid succession.

'That'll bring every Apache in the territory here,' Luke said as the Indian's fusillade echoed out over the wilderness.

They remounted their horses. Luke and the Navajo rode from the waterhole, but Apaches attracted by the explosive sound of gunfire lined the edge of the mesa behind them. Then four others emerged from the timber on the rim ahead. They exchanged gunfire with the rim riders, killing one. Glancing over his shoulder, Luke glimpsed at least a dozen Apaches raising dust as they rode down the mesa slopes.

They were in a deadly crossfire now as bullets blasted at them from the timber in front and the mesa slope behind.

Riding hard, they reached a dry creek bed as slugs ricocheted off its dry stones. Three Apaches stormed down from the timbered rim, anxious to be first in for the kill. Luke shot the foremost rider clean out of his cloth saddle while Shiye turned his gun to fire at the bunch pouring off the mesa. Hot lead peppered the creek bed. White-eyed with fear, Shiye's pony reared and dumped the Navajo over the creek bank.

Shiye clawed his way up, facing the oncoming riders.

'Blood Knife!' the Navajo yelled. 'He is leading them! We need to kill him – it's our only chance!'

It was as if Blood Knife had heard him. The Apache chief slowed his pony, exhorting his warriors before urging them to ride past him and charge the dry creek where the invaders of his territory were holed up. Stirred up by Blood Knife's oratory, the Apaches stormed forward at the same time as the riders coming down from the rim opened fire again.

Shiye squinted down the barrel of his rifle.

'Wait,' Luke told him.

'Blood Knife is mine. I have been searching for him for many moons. He disgraced my mother and he disgraced our family,' the Navajo declared hoarsely as a bullet whistled past his left ear. 'He is mine to kill.'

'But use my gun,' Luke said, passing his Sharps rifle to him. 'It's a helluva lot more accurate and shoots three times as far as your old hunting gun.'

Shiye grabbed the Sharps rifle with grateful hands while Luke, crouched beside him, began pumping his Peacemaker. Bullets raked the creek bed as the Apache riders loomed closer.

Seeing a space between the charging Apaches, the chief's son drew a careful bead on the man he and all the others in his Armijo clan hated.

He aimed straight at Blood Knife's chest and pulled the trigger.

The rifle thundered and bucked against the Navajo's shoulder.

Blood Knife clutched the right side of his chest where blood was gushing through his Mexican tunic, slumped over his pony's head and toppled sideways into a sage bush.

An old Apache brave, who had claws secured around his neck with a leather cord, let out a piercing yell, drowning out the war whoops that faded into silence. Not another shot was fired. Warriors leapt from their ponies and ran back to their fallen chief, making a ring around him. Then the old man with the claws began to sing a mournful dirge that rose high above the rims and the mesa.

'The death song of the Apaches,' Shiye explained, handing the Sharps rifle back to Luke. 'Their chief, Blood Knife, is dead. They are angry, very angry. They will try to track us down and scalp us, but right now there is something more important on their minds. First, before they do anything, they must obey Apache custom.'

'Which means sending his spirit to the Happy Hunting Grounds?' Luke figured, remounting Buck.

Shiye nodded gravely. 'This will not take long. They will make sure of that. Then, Luke Dawson, they will come for us.'

'In other words, we get the hell out of here,' Luke said.

'Well said,' the Navajo agreed.

The Apaches who'd been staked out on the timbered rim were riding across the flat now to join their blood brothers. Their eyes were loaded with bitter hatred and desire for revenge as they rode across the dry creek bed. They couldn't wait to kill the white man and the Navajo but the religion of their ancestors demanded that Blood Knife's spirit be released first. One of them was almost tempted to disobey the beliefs that had been ingrained in him since childhood, but the rider alongside him uttered a guttural warning and the moment passed.

'Ride,' Luke said under his breath.

They headed together along the creek bed until they were out of sight of the Apaches. The death song still rose, eerie and wavering, like the cry of a ghost, as they drew rein under an arrowhead pine.

'I will ride back and tell my father of Blood Knife's death,' the Navajo told him. 'There will be rejoicing. And when the soldiers come from Fort Beaver, we will be safe from any Apache murder raids.'

'Also tell him to prepare to return to the Armijo land in Sundown Valley,' Luke said.

'I hope this will be so, Luke Dawson, my friend.' The Navajo chief's son added, 'We fight well together, Luke Dawson. I could still help. I want to help you. You saw I can shoot straight! Once I tell my father the news, I can ride swiftly to Sundown Valley and be alongside you.'

'Thanks for the offer, but from now on this is my game,' Luke said.

'Are you sure?'

'Shiye, you said the Apaches will not take long with their

religious duties,' Luke reminded him. 'I suggest you and me both ride now, I'll go to Sundown Valley, you to Na Dené Canyon.'

The Navajo grinned as he quoted Luke, 'So we get hell out of here?'

'Right now,' Luke said. He spoke in the Navajo tongue, 'Ya'at'eeh, my friend.'

'See you later,' Shiye confirmed.

Luke headed Buck away, his eyes fixed on the twin peaks that overhung Whispering Pass. He turned in the saddle just once to make sure Shiye rode unharmed past the wailing Apaches.

Satisfied his Navajo friend was safely well on his way, Luke rode into the wilderness.

CHAPTER ELEVEN

Luke rode all day, then the next, resting two nights without a campfire. On the third morning he left Whispering Pass behind and took the trail he knew down through the pine forest. He reached the widow's cabin. Rose was milking her cow and she waved briefly to him as he rode by. Minutes later, the trail took him to Wishbone's place. Even as he rode into the clearing, the door burst open wide and Annie came running out.

As Luke slid from the saddle, she rattled off, 'Thank God you're back safe and well. You shouldn't have ridden all that way after having that bullet cut out of you. Luke, I was so worried—'

'And she was, too, Luke,' Wishbone greeted him from the doorway. 'You were on her mind day and night. Reckon there must be a reason.'

Annie's cheeks flushed crimson at her father's words. She warned him, 'Pa! Careful what you say, Pa!'

'I had to make that ride,' Luke said.

'Yes, I know,' she agreed. 'I was just so worried, that's all.' Eyes shining, Annie invited him in. 'Coffee pot's warming on the stove.'

'Yeah, we need to have a talk,' Wishbone told him.

'I could use that coffee, Annie, but it'll be just a real short talk,' Luke said. 'Five minutes, no more.' He explained, 'I have business to attend to.'

'I reckon you might have, too,' Wishbone agreed. Then the trapper told him in a cryptic tone, 'There's something you need to know, but first, tell us what happened with you.'

Luke filled them both in as he drank Annie's home-brewed coffee and munched her freshly baked cookies. Wishbone and his daughter listened in silence. Annie was white-faced and couldn't help but let out a few sobs while Luke told them about the Sundown Valley massacre. However, they were relieved and thrilled to learn that a few Navajos had survived. Even the hardened old trapper shed more than a tear when Luke let them know Chief Nastas now had his hero son's Medal of Honour in his safe keeping.

He concluded with, 'Had a brush with Blood Knife on the trail home but Shiye, the chief's last remaining son, took care of him. Tell you about it later.' He downed the last of his coffee and prompted Wishbone, 'You said there was something I should know?'

'Yeah, reckon so,' Wishbone said, retrieving a cigarette he'd half-smoked from its ashtray. He relit the cigarette in the warm ashes of the potbelly stove. 'Been having trouble with a pesky bobcat. Killed my turkey I was raising for Thanksgiving. Trailed the varmint yesterday. Tracks led along Wild Wolf Ridge, right by your place and when I rode past, I noticed something different.' He drew on his cigarette. 'Your fence had been fixed. I saw new wire, some new posts, even a new gate by the trail.'

'There's more,' Annie recalled what her father had told her. 'Pa saw riders on your land.'

'It was close to sundown, dusk, so I couldn't see them clearly, but I'd swear on the Good Book they were Triple Z men. One was the Irishman, O'Neill. I'm sure of that. The other, well, can't be too sure but I reckon he looked like Heck Halliday. They were roaming your land real casual like, just as they would on Zimmer's Triple Z range.'

'Pa came home and said it was like the Triple Z had taken over your spread,' Annie remembered.

'Because they thought I was buzzard-bait,' Luke figured grimly, imagining what the back-shooting Halliday must have told his boss on his return from the outlaw canyon. 'Well, thanks to you, Annie, I'm not only still breathing but I'm aiming to right some wrongs.'

'Sounds like fighting talk,' Wishbone said seriously.

Luke shrugged. 'Thanks for the coffee, Annie.'

'Zimmer's a mighty powerful man and he has many guns on his payroll,' Wishbone said, stubbing his cigarette into the ash tray, then hesitated before adding bravely, 'but I'm willing to ride with you.'

Luke looked at Annie's father. He was an old man who meant well. Wishbone had been a good, useful sidekick when he rode to investigate those shots on the first night he was here, but the mission he was on now was different, very different. Besides, Wishbone deserved to live out his remaining years in peace.

'You'll stay right here with Annie,' Luke said flatly.

'Hell's bells, Luke! You can't take on Zimmer and his whole flamin' outfit on your own!' Wishbone protested.

'I aim to try.'

Luke stood up, leaving Wishbone to shake his head in

sheer disbelief. Annie followed Luke to the door, then to his waiting horse.

'I know why you have to do this,' she said tremblingly, 'so I won't try to talk you out of it.' She smiled. 'You wouldn't listen anyway.' After he'd mounted Buck, she reached up and clasped his right hand in both hers. 'Come back to me because I love you, Luke Dawson.'

With her passionate declaration ringing in his ears, Luke rode out of Wishbone's clearing and headed for his own Bar LD spread. He took the narrow track that threaded down through pines and mossy logs to the track that followed his fence line. The sun warmed him when he emerged from the forest.

The fence was indeed fixed. There were no coils of wire in the grass, no strands hanging from fence holes, no gaps. The post he'd seen uprooted when he'd first come back from the war had been hammered back into the soil and the gate's rusty hinges had been replaced with shiny silver ones. He halted Buck under a low-slung pine branch and looked out over his Bar LD range.

That's when he saw movement. Steers! About a dozen brown beeves grazing on his land, just north of his cabin. He looked hard at the closest steer. Big, brown, with patches of white, with the Triple Z brand burned darkly into its hide. He knew for sure now. Trusting Heck Halliday's word that the former Union soldier was dead, the greedy Dallas Zimmer had acted to simply take over the Bar LD spread, adding to his growing empire of land.

Then, as Luke remained in the saddle under the sheltering pine, he saw a rider on a lanky grey horse. Cold anger gripped him as he watched the man drifting slowly, almost nonchalantly, through the small herd. Luke recognized him. He was one of the two Mexicans he'd seen riding with Zimmer when the Triple Z crew had challenged Honani and himself on that first day they'd returned to Sundown Valley. He wore an oversize sombrero, white shirt, black pants and two guns. The Mexican had obviously been given the job of looking after the initial herd to graze here. He was whistling like he didn't have a care in the world.

Luke urged Buck to the gate, leaned over and lifted the iron catch.

He booted the gate open, lifted his Peacemaker and rode on through.

Hearing the gate smack hard against the fence, the Mexican halted his grey gelding and looked over the steers at the incoming rider. Brimming with rage, Luke charged straight across the grass. The Triple Z cowhand stared at Luke like he'd seen a dead man. Tentatively, he jerked his left hand down towards a holstered Colt .45, but seeing Luke's levelled gun, he panicked. The Mexican's fingers froze, dangling mid-air as Luke's bay horse barged through the beeves and came to a snorting standstill beside him.

'Don't shoot me,' the Mexican rider pleaded.

Luke demanded, 'What the hell's going on, greaser?'

'Sorry, sorry!' the Mexican wailed.

'This is my land, you're trespassing.'

'Pedro obey Señor Zimmer, just do job for paydirt,' the rider pleaded.

'Well, you listen, greaser, and listen good,' Luke said slowly.

Pedro the Mexican nodded. '*Sí, sí*, I listen.'

'Ride back to your boss. Give him my thanks for fixing

the Bar LD fences, my fences.' Luke Dawson then added slowly and coldly, 'Give the filthy snake the message that I'm about to come calling. Tell him he's about to pay for arranging those outlaws to commit the cold-blooded murder of Lance Corporal Honani. He'll also pay for bringing along a bunch of killers and a Gatling gun to massacre the Navajo people. And that's just for starters.'

The Mexican's jaw dropped. He warned, sternly now, 'Do not come calling! Stay away! Señor Zimmer will not like you spoiling his big day. Today he marries his señorita.'

Luke stared at the Mexican. He didn't ask Sierra when the wedding would take place. All he remembered was she had said it was in less than two weeks. He'd had too much on his mind to count the days but he figured it'd been ten, maybe eleven days since he'd spoken with her. So the scheming, murdering bastard would be wed today.

He thumbed back the hammer of his Peacemaker. The Mexican whimpered in fear as he heard the sharp, metallic click.

'Where? The ranch house?'

'No,' Pedro replied, shaking. 'Spanish Wells.'

'Go there now and tell him I'm riding in to settle our score.'

'*Sí, señor*, I ride,' the Mexican cried, sweat running down his olive face.

'Now!' Luke snapped.

Pedro wove through the milling beeves and rode hell-for-leather towards the open gate. Luke watched him as he galloped along the fence line, heading for the slope that led into Sundown Valley, and the trail to Spanish Wells.

Dallas Zimmer selected and lit a fat Turkish cigar from the

ornamental box, a pre-wedding gift from the town mayor. He was standing in front of a wardrobe mirror in the main bedroom on the first floor of the Spanish Wells Hotel that he owned, just one of his growing chest of assets. It was here, in room one, where he was changing into his new pinstriped suit, designed by a Philadelphia tailor especially for his wedding to Sierra Cooper.

He imagined his bride putting on her wedding dress now, getting ready in her home, which after today she wouldn't need; she'd be his wife living in the Triple Z ranch house. He buttoned up his white shirt, then buckled his leather belt. Looking again into the mirror, Zimmer had to admit he was much older than Sierra, but that didn't matter. Grinning, he glanced at the four-poster bed they'd share tonight. It wouldn't be long now before she'd be his.

The Gospel Chapel's bell began to ring, reminding the town that Mr Dallas Zimmer's wedding was going to take place in one hour. Not that the folks of Spanish Wells needed reminding. The marriage had been front-page news in the latest edition of the Clarion. Two canvas banners on ropes had been hung across Main Street. There were posters on the town noticeboard, at the school, in the saloon, even in the perfumed Blue Room. In addition, Fenwick had agreed to paste one in his store window. Everyone knew.

Not everyone was invited to the wedding, of course, but there would be ample onlookers and well-wishers. Brother Cain and his fancy lady had come all the way from Tombstone City. Zimmer's son George had taken the day off from the law office, leaving Deputy Kel Drake in charge. Zimmer frowned once more when he thought about Drake. The Methodist lay preacher was far too narrow-minded as far as he was concerned. Maybe one day he'd have to be edged out, but that would wait. There were more important things to think about, like putting a ring on Sierra's finger and then plundering her in this hotel room as soon as the nuptials and supper were over.

He heard the thunder of hoofs. Glancing out of the window, he looked down on Pedro Rodrigo, one of his Mexican riders, raising dust as he rode hard down the centre of Main Street. He frowned. Hadn't he ordered the greaser to stay and mind the steers on his new slab of land on Wild Wolf Ridge? He shrugged, making a mental note to get O'Neill to remind the Mexican to obey orders.

Pedro halted his horse right below his balcony window. The Mexican almost fell in his haste to dismount. Even from his room, Zimmer heard the frantic drumming of boots on the wooden boardwalk, then the sudden sound of a door being wrenched open and slammed shut. The rancher blew cigar smoke as the urgent sound of raised voices, one belonging to Pedro, the other being O'Neill's, penetrated up through the floorboards of his room. Boots pounded the staircase and when Zimmer threw open his door he saw O'Neill and the Mexican standing there. The Irishman's face was set grim while Pedro Rodrigo was puffing and blowing like a railroad engine going uphill.

Zimmer demanded, 'What the hell's going on?'

'Pedro brings bad news,' the ramrod said.

'Well, spill it! I don't have all damn day!' Zimmer reminded them, 'I'm getting hitched in less than an hour's time.'

'It's Dawson,' O'Neill spoke for the Mexican. 'He's still alive.'

'He can't be,' the rancher said hoarsely. 'Heck shot him dead.'

'Men like Dawson don't die easy,' O'Neill said. He suggested, 'Maybe Heck just winged him and he survived.'

'Heck was sure he was dead,' Zimmer insisted, dropping his cigar.

O'Neill shrugged. 'With men like Dawson you need to make sure, and knowing Heck Halliday, he didn't hang around to check.' He sneered derisively, 'We both know he's a yellerbelly.'

'Look, I'll deal with Dawson later,' the cattle baron said, shrugging dismissively. 'He's not gonna spoil my wedding day.'

'I reckon he might, Mr Zimmer,' O'Neill said quietly. 'Tell him, Pedro.'

The rancher's face turned ashen as the Mexican recalled his meeting with Luke Dawson. Eyes narrowing to dark slits, blue veins standing out on his temples, Dallas Zimmer listened to every stammering word uttered by his nervous rider. So Dawson knew about the Navajo massacre. He knew about his former liaison with Scurlock's outfit. Zimmer regretted sending the Mexican to his new land on Wild Wolf Ridge. He should have given the chore of minding the steers on the Bar LD to Ramrod O'Neill. The Irishman would have simply shot Dawson dead as he rode across his grass. But this was no time to nurse regrets. Luke Dawson was coming to settle the score. He told himself a man like Dawson who knew too much had to be silenced one day, so it might as well be now. Damn inconvenient, though.

'Pat,' the rancher addressed his ramrod, 'seeing as Luke Dawson's on his way in to town, we need to take care of him

146

once and for all.'

'I'm with you, Mr Zimmer.'

'First, call on my bride, Sierra,' the rancher told him. 'Just tell her the wedding's off for today, postponed till next week, because I have important business to deal with.'

'Miss Cooper won't like that, Mr Zimmer,' the ramrod warned, raising his shaggy eyebrows.

'Just tell her our future's at stake,' the rancher said. He added, 'A woman who's about to be queen of my empire will understand such things.'

O'Neill was dubious about that. 'Well, OK.'

'And let the preacher know too,' Zimmer added.

'Uh, sure, boss.'

'Then get the boys together,' Zimmer ordered his ramrod. 'They're in town for the wedding, but instead we'll turn it into a funeral for Luke Dawson. Tell them to strap on their holsters, load their guns and get here to this hotel pronto.' He vowed darkly, 'We're going to fill the interfering polecat with lead and bury him before sundown.'

'Leave it to me,' O'Neill assured him.

O'Neill and the Mexican left and tramped back down the stairs.

Dallas Zimmer didn't bother to take off his wedding suit.

Sweating and muttering expletives under his breath, the rancher simply clawed for his leather gun belt.

CHAPTER TWELVE

Nigh noon saw Luke Dawson ride his bay horse across Sundown Valley. An hour later he followed the Triple Z ranch fence line, circled the ancient towering butte and headed through the shadows of Sagebrush Pass. Buck's hoofs were beating a steady drum as Luke emerged from the pass and took the trail that led to Spanish Wells. The morning breeze had dropped right out and the town ahead of him shimmered in the mid-afternoon heat. He rode closer to town limits, following the trail over an old wooden bridge that spanned a tepid creek.

After this, he topped a timbered rise. Spanish Wells was just below him. It was shrouded by an all-pervading silence, like the silence of Boot Hill. Luke saw no movement, no stagecoaches coming in or out of the town, no riders stirring the dust, and so far not even a man or woman on the streets.

He nudged Buck into a walk, taking the dusty road that led past the empty stockyards into town. He reached Buffalo Street. Just ahead, the Confederate flag hung limply on its pole beside Major Wallace's home. Luke gave the flag a cursory glance as he neared Wallace's gate. It was then he heard Wallace's sharp warning.

'The barn! One varmint's staked out in the old barn!'

Luke looked at the disused barn twenty paces down the street. Usually shut and bolted, the old wooden doors were slightly ajar, a thin dark slit between them. He lifted his Peacemaker and fired just as a rifle muzzle protruded. Luke's bullet ripped between the two doors and thudded into flesh and bone. Rodrigo, the Mexican he'd caught on his land earlier today pitched forward, splintering the doors as he crashed headlong between them and lay sprawled in the dust.

The thunder of Luke's shot reverberated over Spanish Wells.

'Thanks, Tim,' Luke called out as the major left his place of concealment on the front porch.

The Confederate major, clad in his old grey uniform, must have abandoned his crutches because he now had the strength to come limping towards him unaided by his wooden props.

'Don't mention it, Luke,' Wallace said, hobbling along the path. Finally reaching the gate, he explained, 'Heard that Irish fella, O'Neill, bawl out at the top of his voice to Sierra Cooper, our neighbour two houses down from here.' He hesitated. 'I reckon you spoke about her that night in the way station.' When Luke remained silent, he continued, 'Well, O'Neill hollered out the wedding was off because they had to take care of you. The whole street heard it. After that, he ordered the greaser to hide over in the old barn and ambush you as you rode on past. Now, I wasn't going to let that happen, not after what you did for Elizabeth and me.'

'Like I said, I'm beholden to you,' Luke said gratefully.

'Hell, they must sure want you dead,' the major said. 'They're staked out all over town just waiting for you.'

'They have their reasons.'

'I used to tell my Confederate soldiers not to ask why, but just fight,' Tim Wallace recalled seriously, 'so I'm not going to ask questions myself.' He declared stoutly, 'I'm riding in with you, Luke.'

Luke retorted, 'This isn't your battle. It's mine.'

'Now you listen to me,' Wallace admonished sternly. 'I'm a Confederate major; you're just a Billy Yank private. My boys might have lost the war but I sure still outrank you. So no goddamn arguments, Private Dawson!' He turned and yelled a command. 'Elizabeth, my horse!'

Responding, his wife led his already-saddled horse from where she'd been holding its bridle ready for Tim's summons. Luke hadn't figured on this. As far as he was concerned, this was his fight and Wallace didn't need to repay him for rescuing his wife from that lecherous swine in the way station. In any case, the major had already done enough by warning him about the Mexican hidden in the barn. However, the Confederate officer was obviously a determined man.

'You sure?' Luke asked.

'Damn sure.'

Luke waited as Wallace painstakingly hauled himself into the saddle. His old wounds still ached and the worried expression on Elizabeth's face betrayed how she felt. Nevertheless, like Luke, she understood.

The two men rode together up the silent street. After they'd passed Sierra's home, the curtains parted and the bride's face was framed between them. Her complexion was as white as the wedding dress she'd just put on.

Luke rode just ahead of Wallace and reached Main Street. There were no boardwalk loungers. In fact, the street looked deserted. No horses were tethered to tie-rails, no piano music floated from the Lucky Deuce. All shops had their doors shut and some were bolted. Only the chapel door remained wide open. Banners inviting everyone to come to the wedding had been taken down.

Dallas Zimmer emerged from the Spanish Wells Hotel and stood under its front balcony. 'Dawson!' Zimmer's bellowing voice echoed out over the silent town. 'Dawson, we need to talk!'

Zimmer seemed to be alone but Luke wasn't fooled. In fact, he glimpsed a shadow high in the chapel belfry and Wallace murmured a warning that further down the street there was a furtive movement between the two stone wells. Furthermore, for no apparent reason, a covered wagon stood across the head of Buffalo Alley.

Luke called back, 'What's on your mind, Zimmer?'

'Let's have a drink like two civilised men.'

Luke told Wallace to keep a watchful eye on the wagon.

'Civilized?' Luke's voice rang out loud and clear over Spanish Wells. 'Do you call wiping out a whole Navajo village civilised? Well, there were witnesses, Zimmer, witnesses to you using a Gatling gun to wipe out women and kids so you could steal their land. You might have killed folks on Wild Wolf Ridge who saw and heard what happened, but there were others you missed. They know your filthy secret, Zimmer.'

'Watch your goddamn mouth, Dawson,' Zimmer yelled.

'Civilised?' Luke repeated as he slid from his horse's back. 'Is that what you call hiring Scurlock's outlaw gang to murder a Navajo war hero just because you thought he

151

might stir up trouble? I'd call it straight out cowardly.'

Realizing half the town was hearing this, Zimmer bristled with fury.

Suddenly he exploded, 'Goddamn Injuns! Who cares about a bunch of goddamn Injuns?'

Luke replied, 'Maybe more folks than you think.'

'Heck! He's yours!' Zimmer called out.

Luke glimpsed the shadow in the belfry become Heck Halliday, who crouched beside the big brass bell with a rifle in his hand.

He whipped up his Peacemaker. 'This one's for Susan.'

Luke fired a single shot that smashed into the deserter's chest, boring through flesh and bone. Halliday screamed, dropped his rifle and clutched the bell. The chapel bell clanged wildly, pealing out over Spanish Wells as Halliday swayed on his heels and finally slipped. The Triple Z hand plunged headlong to the street below where he crunched into the dust.

Rifles poked through slits in the wagon canvas as gunfire rocked the town. Pedro the Mexican was dead by the barn. However, the other Mexican who rode for Zimmer clambered to his feet behind the well by the undertaker's parlour. He lifted two rifles and rested both on the well's stone wall. Simultaneously, O'Neill and the Lucky Deuce's bartender, Blundell, burst through the saloon batwings with guns blazing.

Luke threw himself to the boardwalk as bullets splintered inches from his left hip. There, on the boards, he fired lead into the swaying wagon. Meanwhile, Wallace's Army Colt blasted the Mexican by the well, shattering his shoulder. Yelling in agony, the Mexican sagged over the stone wall, both rifles clattering against the sides of the well before splashing into the water.

Next Luke took care of the bartender, his well-aimed bullet lifting him clean off his feet, blowing his dead body back through the Lucky Deuce's batwings. Meantime, the major backed his horse into Buffalo Street but Luke knew he wasn't retreating. He wasn't that kind of man. Within moments Luke heard the sudden thud of hoofs along Glory Alley. Even as Luke exchanged more gunfire with the Triple Z hands in the wagon, Major Wallace showed up where Glory Alley spilled into Main Street alongside the two wells. Wallace slid from his saddle and hobbled to the nearest well, which he sheltered behind while bullets kicked the street dust by his boots. From there, Wallace started keeping the men in the wagon busy, his bullets shredding canvas, forcing them to drop flat to the wooden floor.

Taking advantage of Wallace having the men in the wagon pinned down, Luke ran across Main Street, his gun blazing. Swearing, Zimmer backed into the hotel but O'Neill stood his ground outside the saloon, levelling his rifle. The Irishman's first bullet whistled past Luke's head and smacked into the law office wall. Still Luke came running at him, his Peacemaker pumping lead. Ramrod O'Neill's second shot winged wide but his third nicked flesh from Luke's left arm, staining his shirt with a smear of blood.

Just as Luke reached the boardwalk, O'Neill backed clumsily towards the saloon batwings. Luke's next two Peacemaker bullets blasted into O'Neill's chest. The Triple Z ramrod pitched sideways, toppling into the saloon window. Dropping his gun, the Irishman fell through the shattered window and crashed headlong into the fragments of glass that littered the floor.

With Tim Wallace keeping up his barrage of flying lead, Luke kept striding towards the hotel entrance. He pushed open the door and saw Zimmer at the top of the stairs, blundering towards his room. The rancher ran into room one and Luke, reloading his Peacemaker, heard the key turn in the lock hole. Luke marched up the stairs. Even as he mounted the staircase, he heard the rancher's frantic summons from the room one balcony overlooking Main Street.

'George! George! Where the hell are you, boy?' Dallas Zimmer's booming voice rang out over the town. 'You're the sheriff, so come out and arrest the bastard. Come out now!'

Luke reached room two.

He turned the brass handle and looked inside.

This was the room where O'Neill and two others had been changing ready for the wedding. Clothes were strewn all over the bed and hung over chairs but no one was in the room. He walked inside, closed the door and headed to where the room opened out onto its own balcony. Like room one's balcony, it jutted out over the street. Zimmer was still on his balcony, bawling out to his sheriff son at the top of his voice. In fact, Zimmer's urgent orders were all that could be heard. Even the guns on Main Street had fallen silent.

Stepping out on to his balcony, Luke had his reloaded Peacemaker aimed at Dallas Zimmer. The rancher didn't see or hear him. He just kept raving at his badge-toting son, imploring him to come out of the safety of his law office and do his duty.

'Zimmer,' Luke called him.

The rancher froze. He stood sideways to Luke, looking

154

straight across the street at the law office door. He was clutching a six-shooter in his right hand, the gun pointing to the balcony floor. With drops of sweat beading his brow, the Triple Z rancher jerked his head around and stared at Luke, who was just a few feet away.

'You've got the drop on me, Dawson,' Zimmer said hoarsely.

'Reckon I have, Zimmer,' Luke agreed. 'You gave those Navajos no chance. It was straight-out murder. But, I'm going to give you a chance you don't deserve.' His tone was soft but cold as death itself as he commanded, 'Put your gun back into its leather, nice and slowly, and I'll do the same. Then, Zimmer, I'll count to three.'

Sweat dripped down Zimmer's cheeks and jaw.

'Okay, I agree,' he croaked. 'I'll sheath my gun.'

Luke watched him like a hawk.

Zimmer hesitated, then slowly turned his whole body to face him squarely while at the same time lowering his gun inch by inch towards its holster.

Luke slipped his Peacemaker right back into its leather, waiting.

Seizing his opportunity, Zimmer edged his gun right to his holster, looking like he was going to slide it in . . . until the last moment. Suddenly the rancher whipped his gun into play but Luke was ready for him. Clearing leather, Luke fired a single bullet from his hip, blasting a hole clean through the rancher's heart, dropping him to the balcony floor. There, Zimmer lay face down, blood soaking his wedding shirt, one puffy finger curled lifelessly around his trigger.

With Zimmer dead, the Triple Z hands in the wagon yelled out that they'd had enough. The wagon shook as one by one they jumped down, watched by Major Wallace who held his rifle while still keeping a wary eye on them.

Luke ran back through room two and down the stairs where he met Wallace on the street. The Triple Z men had left their guns in the wagon and stood with their hands high in the air. After a brief word with Luke, the major dismissed them like he would soldiers on parade. Glad to be alive, they ran for their horses.

'Zimmer was a low-down, sneaky sidewinder to the end,' Wallace remarked on the rancher's final attempt at deception. 'But you were faster anyway.'

'Couldn't have done it without you, Tim.'

'Luke, behind you,' Wallace warned. 'Law office.'

Turning, Luke saw the door inch slowly open. Luke expected to see Sheriff George Zimmer looming behind a gun but instead he saw the town's silver-haired deputy, Kel Drake, who'd once bought a horse from him before the war. He remembered reducing the price for the dour Methodist so he could afford his circuit riding. There was no gun in Drake's hand as he came towards them. He was a man of few words, except in the pulpit when he was known to preach one-hour sermons.

'Sheriff Zimmer was about to open the window and shoot you in the back when you crossed the street,' Drake said. 'I've known for a long time that Zimmer and his son were involved in evil. I turned a blind eye for far too long. May God forgive me! Today I figured it was about time I did more than just preach righteousness. I did something. I stuck my gun into George's back, took his rifle and marched him to a cell. The court will deal with him.'

Luke shook hands with him. 'I'm beholden to you, Kel.'

Doors were opening; folks were beginning to come out

on Main Street. A whiskery old timer started sweeping glass from the front of the Lucky Deuce and Undertaker Uriah Kemp, rubbing his hands together, came striding down the street with tape measure in hand. Spanish Wells was returning to normal. Luke thanked Tim Wallace once again, promising to call when he next came to town.

As Luke made ready to ride, Deputy Drake stood outside the law office.

'See you in church,' the Methodist invited.

There was a wry smile on Luke's face. 'Maybe.'

He rode back down Buffalo Street.

Sierra, still in her wedding dress, was on the front porch.

When she saw Luke, she ran to her fence. Her eyes were red, her face wan but she was strangely composed.

'I did what I had to,' Luke said quietly.

'I know,' Sierra acquiesced. Eyes downcast, she admitted, 'Dallas wasn't a good man. I just liked the notion of being Mrs Sierra Zimmer but I made a mistake. A big mistake. I'll learn a lesson from this.'

Luke acknowledged her with a brief nod.

As he kept riding, she followed him inside her fence and suggested, 'Luke, later, when this all settles, if you'd like to come calling, I wouldn't say no.'

'So long, Sierra,' Luke said, heading for Sundown Valley.

It was a week later when Luke Dawson stood under the big arrowhead pine where his brother had lost his life. He looked down over Sundown Valley. Cain Zimmer, having inherited the Triple Z from his brother Dallas, had acted with speed, hired more hands and removed all of the cattle back to the ranch. He didn't intend to have a fight with

Luke Dawson so that's where they'd stay.

The Navajos had returned. Here, on the edge of Wild Wolf Ridge, Luke saw the three new hogans they had just built on the same grass where their village had been destroyed. Soldiers from Fort Beaver had escorted the last members of the Armijo clan safely across Apache territory, leaving them here to start a new life. There was only a handful but the tribe would grow.

He heard Annie's footfall behind him.

'That blueberry pie's baked and waiting,' she told him.

She'd been cooking for him daily, visiting the new cabin he'd raised over the remains of the old one. She'd been helping too, proving pretty handy with the hammer and nails. Today she wasn't wearing what she usually had on. The deerskin blouse and pants had been replaced with a home sewn blue cotton blouse and matching dress. Luke stood there wide-eyed. He didn't need to say a word because Annie knew he was admiring her.

'Made them myself, same as the blueberry pie that'll get cold if you don't come inside now,' Annie coaxed him.

But he needed no coaxing. They walked together through the tall grass and ferns, past the half a dozen new horses he was getting ready for breaking in. They entered the cabin, he sat down and she began to slice the pie.

'Been thinking, Annie,' Luke said seriously.

'So have I,' she said, her shiny eyes meeting his over the table.

'You're spending a powerful lot of time here on my horse ranch.'

'I know,' Annie said. She chuckled. 'Widow Rose told me certain folks are talking about us.'

'I'd like to give them something to really talk about,'

158

Luke said.

'Oh?'

He pulled her to him and kissed her long and hard. 'Deputy Drake said he'd like to see me in church. Been thinking about that. Been thinking about going to church . . . and having you stand beside me in front of the preacher.'

'Yes, Luke, yes,' she cried happily.

Annie came into his arms again, and by the time they came to eat the blueberry pie it needed a lot of reheating on the potbelly stove.